Reluctant Heart

"Love Triangles Are Complicated."

By Melisant Scott

Melisant Scott

RELUCTANT HEART

© March 21, 2012 Melisant Scott

OPEN WINDOW PUBLICATIONS, Texas, USA.

888.204.4144

ISBN: 0615615678   ISBN-13: 978-0615615677

13 12 11 10 9 8 7 6 5 4 3 2 1 0 0 0 0 0 0 0

Introduction

Lisa Franklin received her degree in journalism from UCLA and plans to pursue a career as a reporter for the Los Angeles Times. Her life was dramatically altered when she's summoned to Houston after her father's untimely death. She inherits his advertising company and meets two good-looking men – Randall and Steven. Steven is gentle, kind and attentive, whereas Randall is arrogant and a confirmed bachelor. Lisa has childhood hang-ups influenced by an embittered mother. Randall Barryman, the "Golden Boy," makes a play for Lisa at a fund raiser. Lisa's excited at first, then embarrassed and confused when he later disappears. Lisa is torn by indecision whether to continue as a reporter or take-over her father's advertising firm.

Pondering the whirl-wind changes of her life, Lisa plans a trip to Padre Island. An intruder is the last thing she expects. Lisa is awakened by a noise downstairs, and she creeps out of bed. As the front door opens, she hears a sound as if someone hit the wall and muttered incomprehensible words. The intruder moves down the hallway and turns the corner, then Lisa swings a rolling pin. The interloper falls to the floor and she rushes into the kitchen, grabs some rope and flips the lights on. The interloper is lying face down on the rug. He's a big man, she thought as she tied his hands and feet. After considerable effort she manages to turn him over. Lisa almost drops to the floor in shock, it can't be!

"Randall, Randall!" she exclaimed. "Can you hear me?"

No response followed, he was out cold.

Depressed, Lisa buries herself in her work after no word from Randall for a month after the trip to Padre Island. Steven declares his interest in Lisa. The situation is complicated further when Randall hires Franklin Advertising to do promotional work for his firm. Lisa begins a relationship with Steven after a brief, torrid affair with Randall. Their paths cross time and again, igniting sparks. Randall learns of Lisa and Steven's involvement through a childhood sweetheart.

A month and half after the trip to Padre, Lisa is cornered by Randall in her office. Lisa considered his timing odd, because Steven just happened to be out of town on business. Randall insists Lisa accompany him to a job site in California. The trip to California only works to create a greater wedge between them. Bewildered, she accompanies Steven to his sister's wedding in Austin and learns what a happy family is all about. In addition, Steven presses Lisa to commit to a relationship.

Randall has issues of his own. He enjoys his life with Lisa and is miserable without her. Could this be what they describe as love? How can he be sure? Randall enters the picture once, again. What was Lisa to do?

Melisant Scott

Melisant Scott

DEDICATION

I dedicate this book to my husband, who has been supportive and an inspiration in my efforts of writing. His encouragement helped me to write this contemporary romance about a love triangle. Everyone knows triangles are complicated -- somebody wins, and somebody loses.

Melisant Scott

CONTENTS

14 13 12 11 10 9 8 7 6 5 4 3 2 1 0 0 0 0

Melisant Scott

Melisant Scott

ACKNOWLEDGMENTS

My special thanks to the book publishers of the romance genre such as Harlequin Romance, Avon Books, Mira, and Random House, just to name a few which have provided hours of delightful contemporary romance reading which is my favorite, my husband, family and my delightful cats who love me no matter what, I wish to extend my gratitude.

Melisant Scott

CHAPTER 1

"Although red as a lobster, you're beautiful," a familiar voice woke her. Lisa lifted her sunglasses and recognized Steven.

"What time is it?"

"Twelve o'clock."

"Oh no!" Lisa exclaimed, bolting from the chair. Pain reminded her to replace her straps. She had slept in the sun for an hour and a half after her swim and was sunburned. Steven tried to hide a chuckle.

"Hasn't anyone warned you of the hazards of the sun without a sunscreen?" he questioned, attempting to appear serious.

"If there's anything I dislike, it's a know-it-all!"

Steven laughed.

"What brings you out this way?" Lisa asked casually, pushing to her feet.

"I wanted to see you again." His eyes were full of male appreciation in their perusal of her body.

Lisa managed a half-smile as her face colored. "If you'll excuse me? I have to change."

Steven nodded. "I need to speak with Louise." Presently the housekeeper stepped onto the patio, gesturing for Steven to accompany her into the house. He turned, leaving Lisa to stare after him.

Climbing the stairs, Lisa recalled the myriad of emotions that overwhelmed her yesterday in the lawyer's office.

"For those who arrived late, I'm John Forbes, attorney for the late Jeremy Franklin. Shall we begin?"

Lisa's eyes scanned the unfamiliar faces around the conference table. A woman in black was seated to the left of Mr. Forbes. She must be Dora Franklin.

Mr. Forbes continued as Lisa's mind began to reel. How could her father die now?

Life's unpleasant happenings certainly presented all at once. A short time ago life was happy, then Tim ended their relationship. Her grandparents, Lucas and Beverly Owens attended her graduation from UCLA. With a degree in journalism, she planned to continue as a reporter at the Los Angeles Times.

"Lisa, Lisa!"

She looked up as her name called a second time interrupted her reverie. She missed the reading of the will and was the only one at the table. A small group were engaged in conversation with Mr. Forbes.

"What's wrong?" Louise inquired.

"Nothing," Lisa muttered languidly.

"I'm pleased you attended today. It's been a long time. You were ten years old the last time I saw you. How are you my dear?"

"Overwhelmed. I can't believe this has happened. I regret, I didn't have a chance to tell him how much I loved him."

"Jeremy left the largest portion of his stock in the agency to you."
Lisa gazed up mutely.

"Come, I would like you to meet someone."

Lisa took a deep breath as she rose. Louise placed an arm around Lisa directing her toward the small group in the room. "Steven, oh Steven, step over here please." A tall dark-haired man in a dark suit approached. He closed the distance between them in seconds. A pair of friendly gray eyes held her gaze.

"Steven, this is Jeremy's daughter. Lisa, Steven Alexander, Jeremy's right-hand with the firm," Louise introduced with a motion of her hand in each direction.

"Hello, Miss Franklin." Steven offered his hand. "I wish our meeting was under more favorable conditions."

Lisa felt Steven's strength and warmth in the brief contact, as their hands met. "Thank you, Mr. Alexander."

"Your aunt tells me you are from California," Steven commented, his gaze fixed on Lisa. "I'm sure you're fatigued after your trip,"

"How thoughtless of me. Lisa must be weary after her trip," Louise apologized. "Malcolm will drive us home."

The gray Cadillac pulled into the circular drive of a two-storied English Tudor home.

"You home is lovely," Lisa said, as her gaze scanned the magnificent home.

"I'm fortunate," Louise commented with a smile.

Malcolm stopped the automobile, climbed out and walked around to open Louise's door. While the women entered the house, Malcolm removed Lisa's bags, then carried them inside.

A buxom elderly woman met them at the door. "Hello, Miss Louise. Will you dine at the usual time?"

Louise nodded.

"I have some calls to make, Lisa. Mrs. Murphy will show you to your room."

Lisa inclined her head. "I'll see you later."

At the top of the staircase, the housekeeper led Lisa into the guest room. "Rest for awhile. I'll unpack for you later," Mrs. Murphy stated on her departure.

The room held a definite charm with antique cherry wood furniture and a canopied bed. Nevertheless, Lisa was restless. She freshened her makeup, changed into a navy blue skirt and white pullover, then hurried downstairs and out the front door.

Lisa inherited the advertising firm. What did her father leave Dora Franklin? What was Jeremy Franklin like? Was he the womanizer her mother described? She continued to walk caught in her own reverie.

A tall hedge of oleanders blocked her view as she approached the next intersection. A hard oncoming object knocked Lisa to the ground just as she turned the corner. Everything went dark and fuzzy – she was unable to catch her breath.

A soft voice inquired, "Are you alright?" Her breath came at a slower rate now, she opened her eyes to *Prince Charming* hovering over her. Sun streaked chestnut curls fell in tousled disarray to his collar. His furrowed brows and indigo eyes regarded her with concern. As he stood, Prince Charming towered over her. His attire was not that of a knight, but a navy blue jogging suit with a white stripe down each leg. Where was his horse? Lisa shook her head. Again he questioned, "Can you hear me?"

"I'm fine, just a little dazed." Her eyes focused with effort. The haziness around Prince Charming faded but he did not disappear. He smiled as he helped her to her feet.

"I didn't see you. I was running, the next thing I knew you were on the ground. I was concerned when you passed out. I was about to call for help." He spoke in a soothing tone. Lisa continued to stare at the stranger. Prince Charming smiled, a gleam in his eyes.

Embarrassed, she averted her gaze as her cheeks flushed. "Thank you, I'm fine. No need to concern yourself. Everything happened so fast."

"I'm forgetting my manners, my name is Randall Barryman. I would feel better if you came inside to rest for awhile. I want to make sure you're alright. Would you care for something to drink?" he asked with concern. "I live nearby."

Her legs buckled under as she tried to stand. At that moment, his arms snaked out gathering her to him. Shaken, she could hear the beat of his heart, not sure if the fall or nearness of this stranger affected her. He lifted her in a single motion and purposefully carried her inside a nearby house.

"Mr. Barryman, what happened?" a female voice questioned.

"We collided. Prepare a drink for the young lady. I'll take her into the study," Randall ordered. His authoritative voice brought Lisa from of her daze. Their gaze locked as he leaned over Lisa, and placed a pillow under her head.

A flow of electricity pulsed through her. Was the fall enough to knock what sense she possessed from her? She closed her eyes to rest.

"Drink this." Randall encouraged as he roused her from a dream. Lisa accepted the cold glass and began to sip its contents – iced tea with lemon. It tasted good going down her parched throat.

The iced tea and cool temperature inside the house revitalized her. She sat up and looked around the room. The clock over the fireplace read six-thirty. Startled by the time, she moved to stand. Her legs no longer felt weak. She had to return home before she was missed.

"I see you're feeling better," Randall greeted from the doorway. He had changed into tan slacks with a matching plaid shirt. "You gave me quite a stir."

Gave him a stir, that's a laugh! She was shaken, as a building during an earthquake.

"Yes. I'm much better, thank you. Really, I must go."

"What's your name?" Randall asked as he crossed the room.

"Lisa Franklin."

"C'mon, I'll take you home."

"Thanks for your concern. It's not necessary."

"I insist, that's the least I can do." He grasped her elbow and directed her toward the door. Randall helped her into a green Ferrari and closed the door. "Where do you live?" he asked as he started the powerful engine.

It was a short trip to Louise Martin's home. He pulled into the circular drive just as Lisa blurted, "Stop, here please. I've been enough trouble."

"Will I see you again?" Randall asked as he stopped the car. "I normally don't bowl over the women I meet."

"No. You're very kind. Goodbye," Lisa said as she stepped from the car and strode toward the house. Moments later, the car continued down the street. What an utter fool she had made of herself. She hoped never to see Randall again.

~****~

Lisa clad in sapphire lounging pajamas, tied her wet dark mane into a ponytail. So much for reflecting, she thought. She was anxious to learn what could be so important that Steven had to meet with her aunt. Louise and Steven were in the study when she entered.

" I see you sunburned. How dreadful for you," Louise offered sympathetically. "Lisa, Steven's here at my invitation to discuss business."

"I will leave the two of you alone after lunch," Louise explained. "Lunch is ready, shall we?"

They retired to the study after the noon meal.

Steven began, "It was your father's wish that you take over the company. He held the controlling fifty-one percent of the stock, while the other forty-nine percent belongs to your aunt. I'm qualified to help you with this, as I have worked for the company for eight years and I'm acquainted with all facets of the business. Since your arrival at your grandparents, your father stayed abreast of your activities. He approved of your choice in journalism and he felt that you are the logical choice to head our firm."

8

Shocked, Lisa wanted to respond, but the words froze in her throat. Her father loved her, in spite of her rejection. After Meredith's death, she received a few letters from Jeremy Franklin inviting her to live with him and his new wife. Lisa discarded them without a second thought.

"How do you feel about your inheritance?" Louise asked.

"I'm not sure. Everything's happened so fast," Lisa answered diffidently.

"We're pleased to have you with us," added Steven. Attempting to lighten the subject, "I've noticed, your aunt has taken a new vitality since your arrival." Louise shot Steven a puzzled look.

"Thank you," Lisa said, "My aunt has been a dear." She leaned back against the brown leather sofa.

"So tell me, how's California?" Steven asked.

"Much like Houston, only the humidity is higher here."

"How are your grandparents? Their name is Owens, I believe?" Steven continued.

"Yes, Owens. They are fine," Lisa responded.

"I can't imagine why Lisa preferred West Texas to Houston," Louise interjected. "Jeremy tried to persuade her to come here after her mother's horrible death. Poor thing died in an auto accident."

"I'm sure Steven isn't interested," Lisa said. "Besides, that was long ago."

"You were fifteen," Louise said shifting her gaze skyward. "And stubborn like your mother! But sweet. Meredith became bitter after Jeremy left."

"Your parents were divorced?" Steven inquired. "I assumed Dora was your mother."

"No. My mother was a nurse. She became bitter after my father took advantage of her kind nature," Lisa said waspishly, her eyes riveted on Louise.

"Surely you don't believe the lies Meredith tried to spread?" Louise scolded.

Lisa's jaw clenched as her nails dug into her palms.

"Excuse me. I have to leave," Steven apologized, glancing at his watch. "I have to review before a presentation this morning." He stood up.

"Thank you for coming, Steven," Louise commented as she stood.

"My pleasure, Louise," Steven said, shifting his gaze to Lisa. "Come by the office. I'll show you around and answer any questions you might have."

"Thanks, I will. Goodbye, Steven."

"Bye, Lisa."

After Steven's departure, Louise commented, "We would be lost without him."

Lisa considered it wise to hold her tongue.

~****~

"Drive us around town, Malcolm. I want Lisa to see what Houston has to offer," Louise instructed. "Houston has everything one might desire – art museums, colleges, and several restaurants with every conceivable food one can imagine," she supplied.

An hour later Malcolm drove them to the Galleria. "Let us off at the main entrance of the Galleria. And return in two hours, Malcolm," Louise added.

Lisa shopped in malls previously, although nothing quite like the Galleria. Occasionally she would go inside a shop that captured her interest. Louise seemingly enjoyed the trip to the Galleria. They ended the shopping spree with lunch in a French restaurant.

With achy feet and a grimace, they awaited Malcolm's return. The day was productive. Lisa found a long red strapless, taffeta dress and Louise insisted on paying for the garment.

Saturday night arrived quickly with the earlier part of the week a total blur to Lisa. Her hair was drawn atop her head with ringlet curls that fell to one shoulder. Indeed she was exquisite in the red dress on her descent of the stairs. A pearl necklace and ear rings complemented her attire.

"Here we are," Malcolm stated as he turned off the Cadillac's engine. Climbing from the driver's seat, he opened Louise's door and offered his hand. "I hope the affair is smashing, Miss Louise."

"Thank you, Malcolm. That will be all," Louise dismissed. Lisa followed her to the door.

"Good night," Malcolm said, inclining his head.

Outside the Victorian home, several automobiles lined the drive from Rolls-Royce, Mercedes, Jaguar and Porsche.

"Good evening Mrs. Martin," a middle-age, wiry man greeted. "I'll take your wrap."

"Thank you Giles," Louise replied warmly.

"Everyone's in the ballroom," Giles added. "This way, please."

The atmosphere hummed with conversation and music. Groups of two or three people were scattered throughout the grand dwelling. Everyone appeared to know one another.

Louise's gaze swept the large group and settled on Lena Roberts. "Lena, this is Jeremy's daughter, Lisa."

"How do you do?" Lena Roberts said politely.

"I'm fine, thank you," Lisa responded.

The music had a fifties-sixties flavor. Lisa met several people, she knew she would never remember them all. Louise tired after an hour, just the same she encouraged Lisa to mingle.

A willowy young woman with blonde hair approached arm- in- arm with Mrs. Roberts. The slinky black dress she wore left little to the imagination.

"Lisa, I'd like you to meet Clarissa, my daughter."

"How are you?" Clarissa asked with a haughty gesture of her head.

"Very well. And you?" Rarely Lisa met anyone she disliked from the start, but Clarissa could be an exception.

"I'll leave the two of you to become acquainted," Mrs. Roberts stated as she turned. "Sure you have lots to talk about."

"Has mother shown you around?" Clarissa asked.

"No. I would love a tour."

"Then follow me," Clarissa commented with a gesture of her hand. She began with the front room. "So, what is your line of work?"

"I'm a reporter, " Lisa replied proudly. "What about you?"

"A decorator," Clarissa said with saccharine sweetness. "I've been in business for three years and I'm considering two additional staff positions. The demand had been tremendous, and I simply cannot do everything!"

"Congratulations."

Ignoring Lisa's comment, she forged ahead. "How long do you plan to be in the area? Perhaps we could have lunch?"

"I have two weeks leave from work. I doubt it will take longer."

"Pity. Then, I suppose you're anxious to return to California." Clarissa directed Lisa back to the main group. "I'm sorry but I must help entertain the guests. If you'll excuse me?"

"Please. Don't let me keep you," Lisa replied. She observed that Clarissa preferred the male guests. Clarissa was a goddess, sophisticated, well-educated and an inveterate flirt. She would flash one of her radiant smiles, and men would fall at her feet Lisa mused.

After dinner Lisa was weary. She discovered a table near the patio, where she sat down with a sigh. The music began to lull her into a tranquil mood.

Louise approached and tapped her shoulder. "Lisa, I would like to introduce you –"

"Hello, Lisa. How are you?" Randall interrupted.

"How nice to see you again."

"You've met?"

He inclined his head, a crooked smile played on his face. "May I have this dance?" He offered his hand.

Under half closed lashes, Lisa smiled as she accepted his hand, and rose. One hand slid to the small of her back, as he escorted her to the dance floor. Randall was dashing in his formal attire.

The band began to play a slow love song just as they arrived on the dance floor. She hesitated, but Randall pulled her into his embrace. He was a practiced dancer, easy to follow. She attempted to place distance between them, but his grip tightened at her spine.

His breath whispered behind her ear as he nuzzled his face into her hair. The song ended and a tune with a fast beat began. Lisa was uneasy as his lips brushed sensuously along the nape of her neck, then upward to her jaw. Randall whispered, "Let's leave."

She nodded. Anything to move out of his arms.

Clarissa grimaced when she noticed Randall leaving with Lisa. Randall closed the patio door behind them, as they left the noise of the party behind.

The sultry, July night greeted them as they strolled hand-in-hand beneath a full moon. A considerable distance from the house, Randall stopped and turned to face her.

"Enjoying yourself?"

"Yes, especially since you asked me to dance. How have you been Randall?"

"Not bad. I've wondered how you were."

Trying to change the subject, Lisa asked," What is your line of work?"

"My father owns a real estate development company. We do malls, resort hotels and the like. I've taken on his duties since his diabetes has caused health problems. Your aunt said you're from California. On business or pleasure?"

"Neither." Lisa paused, then continued, "My father recently passed away."

As they continued to walk, she looked up at the moon. "It's so beautiful," she pointed with her free hand, "it's so perfect."

~****~

CHAPTER 2

"The moon pales against your appeal," he remarked huskily. His eyes darkened with desire. She lifted her chin in expectation. Randall's mouth covered hers. His playful nips caused her lips to part. Randall deepened the kiss with an insatiable hunger. His tongue plundered the warm recesses of her mouth as he trailed kisses along the hollow of her neck. Lisa reveled in the heady experience. Her fingers moved through his hair. They clung to one another for a brief moment, then Randall withdrew.

"We should go inside before they send a search party," he said attempting to interject humor. They walked toward the Robert's home without physical contact. Just outside the door, Randall halted, as he ploughed a hand through his hair. "You go ahead. I'm going to have a cigarette," he stated briskly.

She felt rejected and embarrassed. She lifted her chin proudly and entered the patio door. Once inside the powder room, she checked her appearance and applied fresh lipstick. Two women strolled inside, laughing.

"Did you notice how green Clarissa was when Randall danced with the girl in red?"

"She was even greener when they left together. Looks like Clarissa has some keen competition," said another.

"Clarissa knows how to handle it."

Both women continued to laugh as they freshened their hair and makeup, then left as abruptly as they appeared. Relieved she went undetected, Lisa joined her aunt. After what happened outside, Lisa needed a drink to calm her nerves. Just at that moment, a servant passed with a tray of drinks, Lisa took a glass of wine."

"Are you enjoying yourself, dear?"

Lisa downed the first glass and motioned for a refill, heaved a deep sigh and smiled."Yes, I am. I think the affair is a success."

"Hello, Steven," Louise greeted on his approach. "I thought you'd left town on business?"

"That's correct," Steven replied. "However, I finished sooner than expected."

Lisa finished the second glass of wine during her conversation with Steven. Now, she lost her reserved air and laughed freely.

"My lady, would you grant a weary knight this dance?" Steven asked with a warm smile.

"Yes, kind sir." Lisa curtsied.

Steven ushered her onto the dance floor just as a slow tune by Bach began. He dwarfed Lisa by ten inches. He held her at gracious distance, but his eyes never left her.

"You look radiant tonight."

"Why thank you."

They continued to dance and the crowd dispersed. Was it midnight already? She felt like Cinderella at the ball. Tonight she received several compliments and admiring glances. She had not seen Randall since she returned to the party. Lisa tried to forget she felt out of control in Randall's arms. Steven made her feel feminine and desirable. He was attentive, gracious, and a good listener, unlike the men she had known in college, who seemed interested only in themselves.

"Ladies, may I escort you home?" Steven asked as they returned. Lisa hiccupped unexpectedly and tried to suppress a giggle, as her hand moved to cover her mouth.

"How thoughtful. First I must say goodnight to the hostess," Louise explained. "The two of you, wait by the car. I'll be out in a few minutes." Louise shook her head as she walked away.

Lisa was tipsy. Steven's arm encircled her waist. Inhibitions aside, she spun around to face him. Their lips were inches apart."Did you enjoy yourself, Steven?" she purred as she lifted her chin provocatively. Steven cupped her chin in one hand and his head dipped in a friendly kiss. Anxious to see if she would experience tingles, Lisa took the initiative. She stepped on tiptoes and drew him closer. This was all the encouragement he needed. His mouth covered hers in a passionate kiss. Although it was pleasant, to her dismay there were no bells or electrical pulsations. Nearby, voices could be heard. Steven released her, placing distance between them.

"Lisa, I—" Steven did not complete the statement.

She did not miss the increased rise and fall of his chest. His gaze searched hers. Blushing, Lisa averted her gaze to the entrance of the house. Louise descended the steps and approached. Steven helped Lisa into the front seat and closed the door. Louise took a back seat.

Lisa saw a small light through the nearby trees as Steven helped her into the car. Was this her imagination playing tricks? she wondered.

The trip to the Martin home was made in silence. On arrival, the Acura pulled into the driveway and stopped. Louise expressed her gratitude and said goodnight.

"Thank you, Steven for the ride and good company," Lisa said politely. "I'm sure you're weary after your trip and all."

"How about a nightcap?" Steven scolded mockingly. He stepped forward, his gray eyes gleamed mischief.

"Another time, I'm exhausted."

He took her into his arms and kissed her thoroughly. "Night, Lisa. I'll see you later."

He made it sound like a promise. She hadn't considered the consequences of her actions. The wine took over where her common sense failed her. For a moment, she leaned against the door after his departure. Surely she would toss and turn, but within minutes, she was asleep.

~****~

Absorbed in thought, Lisa lay in bed the next morning. She regretted her wanton behavior. What was it about Randall that made her feel a sense of danger? He was ruggedly handsome and she was convinced he could command any situation. Instincts warned her he was not to be trusted.

Certainly, he could have any woman he desired. No doubt, Clarissa was interested in him. He seemed to compel one to a point, until he manifested an aloofness that bordered indifference. Women were a pastime, to be discarded when he tired of them. Why did she care? Forget him a tiny voice spoke. If you fancy a man, someone like Steven would be a wiser choice –solid, reliable and handsome. She didn't want or need a relationship, she had enough problems.

The question remained should she take over her father's advertising agency or return to California and resume her career? *Remember why you are here!*

What made Tim break off their relationship? She needed time to think. Was there a flaw in her character she failed to recognize? Tim called her unfeeling, a tease – even frigid, when she found his seduction repulsive! Why? She was supposed to be in love and ready to make a commitment. Was commitment the problem? Perhaps she possessed more of her father's character than she was prepared to admit. Enough! she scolded herself. Get dressed! She would explain the dilemma to Louise, surely her aunt would understand.

Lisa hummed on her descent of the stairs.

Louise was seated in the day room as she entered. "Good morning, Aunt Louise," she greeted cheerfully.

"You're in good spirits."

"It's a beautiful day!" Taking juice, toast and coffee, Lisa busied herself.

"Steven's smitten by you," Louise said. "Could this be the reason for your happiness – in love, dear?"

"No, of course not," Lisa admonished. "What makes you think that?"

"His intense regard as if you were the only woman in the room, made it more than apparent. You realize, he's considered *a catch*! I've never seen Steven react in this manner," Louise added, bewildered. Lisa's pert chin rose. "You're not embarrassed?"

"I think you're making too much of things, really Louise."

"So was everyone in the room."

"What do you mean?" Lisa queried.

"You've created a buzz, everyone's talking. I thought for awhile Randall caught your fancy. The air was charged with electricity as the two of you danced. When you returned alone after leaving with young Barryman, well, your preference pleased Mrs. Roberts. Clarissa has had her sights on him, but somehow he eludes the proverbial noose. The gist of the conversation is that you and Steven will be the next talk of the town."

"I hadn't realized I created such a sensation. I'm glad everyone has it figured out. No one missed a thing!" Lisa said brusquely.

"Why are you so defensive? Steven's a fine young man."

"I'm sorry. Steven's wonderful. But I am not in love with him or with anyone," Lisa said curtly.

"I see," Louise placated.

After breakfast was completed, Lisa's temper cooled. This would be an opportune time. "Aunt Louise, I would like to go away for four or five days. I hope you understand?"

"Yes, indeed. Try the beach house on Padre Island. It's a great place to do some thinking."

"Padre?"

"It's located at the tip of Texas. The beaches are pristine and the water an emerald green. You can drive down in five or six hours.

"Sounds perfect," Lisa remarked. "Have you known Randall long?"

"I have known the Barrymans long before Randall," Louise said, arching a brow with the abrupt turn in conversation.

"He seems aloof," Lisa commented casually, in hope of enlightenment.

"The Barrymans have been prominent in this area for generations. I grew up with Marion Barryman – it was Carlisle, before she married Daniel, Randall's father. She and Daniel planned to travel, however Marion became pregnant. You have to understand, they were not the parental type. When Randall was born, he was reared with nannies and sent to boarding schools. He would come home for the holidays. Poor Randall just seemed to stay in trouble. He was bounced from one school to the next. Marion died three years ago and Daniel's health is poor. He has arthritis and diabetes. Randall lives with his father and oversees Daniel's affairs. Has he said something to offend you?"

"Randall?"

"Yes, of course, Randall," Louise said impatiently.

"No, just curious."

"I suspect a wry expression crossed Randall's face when you danced with Steven. I thought it was my imagination, but seemingly he and Clarissa had a private party on the patio."

He was with Clarissa, that explains it – the rat! She suspected Randall had a ruthless side hidden beneath that charismatic charm. Inside, Lisa fumed.

"I'm relieved to hear that. Randall can be aggressive if he wants something to the point of being manipulative," Louise cautioned. "Never underestimate him. He has a quick temper and is accustomed to having his way. It wouldn't be wise to make an enemy of him. He can be formidable."

"I'll remember that." Lisa tried to lighten the subject. "I'd like to buy a few items for Padre. Care to join me?"

Both women smiled, then turned arm-in-arm to depart. Lisa received a regular income from her father's business, so why not reward herself with a few clothes? She had worked for six years; too proud to accept help any from her father.

Lisa's rental car was now packed with yesterday's purchases, she kissed her aunt goodbye and promised to call on her arrival in Padre. She was clad in tan Capri shorts with an ivory pull-over and at last she was on her way. The eastern sun was luminous. Ordinarily, Lisa was not one to dawdle once she decided a course of action. She stopped three times on the trip to refuel the car, grab something to eat and to answer nature's call. It was now four-thirty. She could see Padre as she approached the long bridge -- the view was picturesque!

The beach house was isolated in a beautiful cove Lisa discovered, when it came into view on the last turn. Great! She removed her baggage from the car, and moved toward the front door. Just as Lisa turned the key in the lock and opened the door, a musty odor overwhelmed her. Seascapes decorated the white walls. The airy earth tones and wicker furniture lent a comfortable atmosphere. It was so quiet here, the only sound was the occasional cry of a seagull and the continuous beat of the waves against the shore. A gentle breeze blew through the windows as Lisa opened them. After unloading the car, Lisa put the groceries away, unpacked her bags and hung her clothes in the closet.

Wearily she sat on the bedside to rest. This would be the perfect hideaway. A few moments later, her stomach began to make noises. She moved into the kitchen, placed an entrée in the microwave to cook, then made a small salad. She had even thought to bring a bottle of merlot to toast her much deserved holiday. Lisa located the wine glasses and poured a glass of the dark, lush wine. The sunset and emerald water beckoned. Lisa moved dinner out onto the patio.

Hypnotized by the sound of the ocean waves as they lapped the shore, tranquility filled her. She discovered the phone was not in order. Thank goodness she had foresight to call Louise earlier.

Bathed and dressed in pink short pajamas, she closed the windows and went to bed. A short time later, she was peacefully asleep.

Awakened by a noise downstairs, Lisa crept out of bed and eased downstairs. She seized a rolling pin from the kitchen then tip-toed to the door. If only the phone worked! Crouched behind a partition that separated the hall and living room, she waited. The front door opened after what seemed forever. The room was in complete darkness. She heard a bang as if someone hit the wall and muttered incomprehensible words.

The intruder moved down the hallway and turned the corner, then Lisa swung the rolling pin. The interloper fell to the floor, and she rushed into the kitchen, grabbed some rope and flipped the lights on. He is a big man, she thought as she tied his hands and feet. After considerable effort she managed to turn him over. Lisa almost dropped to the floor in shock, it couldn't be!

"Randall, Randall!" she exclaimed. "Can you hear me?"

No response followed, he was out cold. Panicking, she rose. She vacillated whether to run outside to yell for help, or just get into the car to go for help. So she paced back and forth in the room.

Alas, calming down, she untied him, propped his feet and covered him with a blanket. Thank goodness, she had had a first-aid course in college. Lisa undressed him until he was clad in just a tee-shirt and briefs then placed an ice pack on his injured shoulder. His breathing and pulse remained regular.

Sponging his face with cool water, she called his name once again. Lisa grew weary after an hour. What if he didn't regain consciousness? Finally, a faint moan, then another, he moved. She continued to sponge his face. Thank heaven! she thought.

"Randall, can you hear me?" Lisa asked with concern. "Are you in pain?"

"Um-ah."

"Randall, it's Lisa, speak to me. Are you alright?

He moaned again, thrashing his head from side to side. Perspiration beaded on his forehead and upper lip. Lisa wiped the perspiration away with a damp cloth. She ran her fingers through his chestnut hair, as if to soothe a child. Again, he moaned.

Randall blinked and opened his eyes as he moved his hand to his head. "Oh, my head," he groaned. "What happened?"

"It's alright, Randall. Please lie still. I thought you were an intruder," she said defensively. "And I hit you with a rolling pin."

"You, what!"

"Can you get up?"

"I'll try," Randall said as he made an effort to sit up. "My left shoulder's killing me. I need a hand up."

When Lisa helped him to sit, she noticed a large lump on his left shoulder. He tried to stand, wavered, then sat down.

"I feel dizzy."

"Just sit for awhile and get used to the change in position," Lisa encouraged. "Would you like some water?"

"Yes, and a couple of aspirin. I have a horrible headache!"

"Lisa left the room and returned moments later with the aspirin and glass of water. Readily he accepted them and leaned back against the sofa.

"When I entered the house, I tried to find the light switch and stumped my toe, then everything went black. You pack a wallop," he said through bleary eyes. "Why are you here?"

"What do you mean?" Lisa countered. "You're the one trespassing!"

"I beg your pardon?" he growled. "My parents and aunt have shared this house for years. I came here to getaway. I had no idea--"

"I am sorry," she commented. "I was so scared, I heard a noise and with the phone out of order."

"Never mind that now, help me up," Randall demanded. Lisa helped him to climb the stairs. She chose a bedroom across the hall from hers, and helped him into bed. His gaze traveled her length, then moved upward to her full bosom. He smiled contentedly as he leaned back.

In her flight, she neglected to put on her robe. There was a clear view down her night gown as she leaned to cover him. No wonder, he was grinning impishly. A flush covered Lisa's cheeks.

"I'll be across the hall. There's no need to worry," she remarked as she bunched the fabric of her night gown in an effort of modesty.

"Thank you. Good night, Lisa."

"Goodnight, sleep well," she answered as she walked out of the room. She left the door open to keep a vigilant watch. He appeared to doze. Lisa disliked surprises, and for good measure she checked the door locks. Glancing out the window, she saw two suitcases on the lighted porch.

~****~

CHAPTER 3

The sun shined brightly into Lisa's bedroom window. She turned her back, covering her head with the sheet. Minutes later, fraught with curiosity, she rose on elbows and glanced into Randall's room. One leg hung from underneath the sheet that covered him to his waist. The ice pack was on the floor. Prone position, he slept.

She slipped on her robe and crept into Randall's room. Now, the lump on his left shoulder was clearly outlined by a large bruise. He appeared comfortable, so she left him to prepare breakfast.

An hour later, Lisa carried a tray into his room. "Good morning, Randall."

He opened his eyes and looked up, then turned onto his back. "Oh, no!" he exclaimed in pain. Placing several pillows behind him, Lisa helped him to sit.

"I'll take care of your shoulder after breakfast." Smiling, she sat the tray on his lap. Lisa prepared coffee, orange juice, eggs and fresh fruit. Randall's tousled hair and the stubble of a day's beard greeted her. "How do you feel?"

"I guess, I'll live." Randall cleared his plate and requested a second cup of coffee. "Breakfast was a welcome sight," he said as she removed the tray. "Thank you."

Lisa pulled a chair close to Randall's bedside, and sat down. "I'm sorry about what happened. I want you to rest for a few days and to watch you closely."

"Are you volunteering? As my nurse?" he asked with a broad smile.

"Yes, since I hit you."

"Say my name?"

"What? Randall?"

"Yes, I like the way you say –"

"Randall," she supplied. Both smiled.

"I'd like some aspirin, my head is throbbing," he commented as he moved a hand to his forehead.

"Right away."

"Thank you, Lisa," he murmured as he leaned against the pillows.

"Rest. I'll help you bathe when your head is better."

While he rested, she would shower, dress and clear the dishes she considered. An hour later, Lisa stood in the doorway to his room. He was staring at the ceiling. "You'll feel better if take a bath. What do you say?"
Randall cupped his chin with one hand. "That has definite possibilities." He shot her an engaging smile. Lisa rolled her eyes in exasperation.

"I'll bring your bags upstairs and we'll start."

A basin of warm water was placed before him. Lisa handed Randall the washcloth, and helped him remove his tee shirt. Cautiously, he washed his face, then moved to his arms and chest. "I'll need some help with my back and legs."

Lisa soaped the washcloth and gently washed his broad back, she took extra care around the bruised area. His body was muscular and firm with powerful arms, she thought. Get a grip! What muscular calves he has. Embarrassed he might read her errant thoughts, she lowered her eyes to avoid his gaze as she positioned the basin before him.

"You finish. I'll return in a few minutes."

Ten minutes later, she found him asleep as if worn out. His jockey briefs joined his tee shirt on the floor. Lisa's heart melted, he looked so vulnerable and downright male, asleep. She changed the basin of water. He woke with a smile.

"Finish the job?" she asked as she handed him clean jockey shorts.

"Aye, aye captain."

"Good. Put on your briefs after I leave. I'll be back shortly to help you shave and do your teeth."

"You're sure bossy," he complained.

Randall was brushing his teeth when she returned. He heaved a sigh and laid the toothbrush down. "You'll have to put up with the beard, I'm worn out."

"Oh, no. I'll shave you," she scolded mockingly.

He leaned against the pillows and closed his eyes with his last statement. Suddenly, he opened them as if stunned.

"It's not that difficult," Lisa reasoned.

The necessary equipment at the bedside, she sat down. Lisa took the razor then applied shaving cream to his face. His eyes followed her movements. This made Lisa self-conscious. The task completed, she leaned closer to check for spots she might have missed.

Abruptly, Randall moved and Lisa fell across his lap. His arms encircled her for support. Gazing into her eyes an extended moment, Randall leaned forward. What began as a playful gesture quickly changed to passion. Willingly, she met his demands. Her pulse and breath quickened.

His breathing became deep. "Lisa ..." Randall speared his fingers through her hair, extending her neck back. Again he kissed her, his tongue probed her warm recesses.

"Randall, I −"

"Oh Lisa, you are beautiful," he whispered sensuously. He held her as if she might disappear. Kissing her throat and shoulder, he unfastened two buttons of her blouse. His hand slipped inside to cup a lace covered mound; his thumb teased each rosy bud with circular movements until it became firm. He released the clasp of her bra. Moaning, his head descended.

A captured erect peak tingled with untold pleasure. Somewhere deep in Lisa's throat a sigh of satisfaction escaped her, as she arched toward him. She was helpless.

"I want you, Lisa," he murmured as he rained kisses along her throat and shoulders. "I want to touch you, to enjoy you touching me." Of their own volition, Lisa's arms wrapped around his neck.

"O-oh!" he rasped in pain as her arm brushed his injured shoulder. Instantly he released her and moved to his right side, groaning.

Responding to his distress, she withdrew. "I forgot about your shoulder," she paused, then continued. "Although it was your fault," she supplied while she fastened her clothes.

"What?" he growled with incredulity.

"Well, if you hadn't kissed me and made me crazy, it wouldn't have happened. I'll get some ice." She darted out of the room.

Lisa tried to regain control. Leaning against the kitchen counter, she released a deep sigh – *that was a close call!* You'll have to be on guard, he's masterful in the art of seduction.

A little voice within her spoke, you should have offered some resistance, even a little, but no, you forgot all reason. Of all people to share a house with, why did it have to be Randall? No man had affected her this way. The chemistry between them was volatile. His touch made her skin feel on fire, it was difficult to breathe, and she thought she heard bells. What control over her did he possess? Did he experience similar sensations?

Remember he's a wolf!

Randall was leaning against several pillows in bed when she entered his room. A devastating smile played on his face. She placed an ice pack wrapped in a towel to his left shoulder.

"Thank you, Lisa."

"Get some rest. Later, I'll look in on you. If you need anything, just call."

"I need you," he teased softly.

"Behave Randall! You know what I mean."

"With you in the house, how can I?" He winked.

"You're impossible." Lisa shook her head on departure.

She would go for a swim and soak up some sun before lunch, she thought. When she stopped by Randall's room on her way out, she found him asleep.

A gentle breeze lifted tendrils of Lisa's black hair off her shoulders. The azure sky and emerald water were beautiful, and the white sand between her toes felt wonderful to Lisa. She felt so alive. Discarding her wrap, she entered the water. Several sea gulls screeched their welcome. The water was warm against her skin. Thirty minutes later, she made way for shore. Laying her towel on the sand, she lowered herself. Sunglasses in place, she closed her eyes and listened to the waves lap the shore. Eventually, she drifted off.

"Lisa, Lisa." Turning, Lisa saw Randall on the patio. He waved. Clad only in bone colored shorts, he was a sight to behold. With a towel in hand, she started back in the direction of the beach house.

"A man could starve to death." A leisurely male appraisal travelled her length."My, you do, fill your suit well."

"Why are you up?" she queried, slipping into her terry wrap.

"I called. When you didn't answer, I decided to investigate," Randall explained. "Enjoy your swim?"

"Yes, the water was fantastic. I'll fix lunch."

"Good idea. I'm starved."

Lisa suspected his hunger was for more than just food. They moved lunch onto the patio to enjoy the panoramic view of the Gulf of Mexico.

"My parents and Louise have always enjoyed the isolation here."

"That's why you're here?"

"Yes." Randall rose and moved toward the water's edge.

The monosyllabic reply suppressed Lisa's urge to pursue the issue.

"How's your shoulder?"

"Sore, but better. This getaway hasn't turned out as I planned. I didn't expect anyone to do me bodily harm." Contemplatively, he stared out to sea.

"I merely tried to defend myself."

Ignoring her words, he forged ahead. "Nor did I expect to share the beach house." A smile replaced the thoughtful expression. "Remind me never to get in your way." His laughter was a rich baritone sound. Randall's relaxed posture was unexpected, although a relief to Lisa.

He had lowered his defenses. Lisa discovered an unfamiliar side of him – perhaps the person, he kept under wraps.

"I remember being knocked breathless to the ground by an interloper," she remarked in the same bantering tone.

"Okay, okay. I give up," he replied, raising both hands in mock surrender. "We're even."

"We'd better go inside. Sunburn won't help either of us."

Once inside the house, Lisa asked, "Do you know if there are any games in the house?"

"Yes, monopoly, scrabble, or cards in the study. Which do you prefer?"

"Scrabble," Lisa suggested.

"You're on."

They played scrabble for the next two hours, laughing and teasing one another. "I haven't played scrabble in years. I'd forgotten what fun it can be," she remarked.

"It was," he agreed wearily. "I think I'll lie down for awhile." Randall stretched out on the sofa. Lisa filled the ice pack and placed it over his shoulder.

"Comfortable?"

Randall moaned through half closed eyes.

He seemed innocent, even boyish. Lisa was determined to avoid a recurrence of this morning's events. Refreshed after a shower, Lisa's gaze settled on Randall as she entered the study. The noise must have awakened him, he moved. Pushing up, he said sleepily, "Hello, Lisa."

"Sleep well?"

"Yes. I would like to thank you for everything," he said.

"You're welcome," she answered. "Care for more tea?"

He nodded.

Lisa joined Randall on the sofa.

"What brought you to Padre, Lisa?"

"I could ask you the same question."

"The constant deadlines at work and my father's in poor health. Occasionally, I feel the urge to be alone, so I come here," Randall explained.

"I'm trying to deal with my father's death and make some decisions," Lisa supplied.

"I'm sorry to hear about your father."

"I didn't know him very well."

"Why not?"

"My parents divorced when I was young. My grandparents raised me."

"I see."

They continued to talk and Lisa felt a camaraderie form between them.

"You seem different, Randall."

"In what way?"

"Oh, more open I suppose."

"Lisa," he said moving closer. "You're an intriguing woman, full of life, so vital." His fingertips stroked her temple and cheek.

Beware! Regardless of the instinctive warning, she ignored it.

"Fate keeps throwing us together," he murmured seductively. His eyes became darkened pools that seemed to penetrate through her.

"Randall, please stop."

"You don't mean that."

"But, I do."

"Lisa, why fight it? I know you're attracted to me."

"We barely know one another." Her voice lacked conviction. He lifted her chin with his thumb. His mouth took possession of hers. Lisa moved her arms carefully around his neck.

"Oh Lisa," Randall whispered. His pulse hammered in his ears.

"Ssh!" Lisa said, placing two fingers across his lips. Moments later they were stretched out on the sofa. Lisa could feel each curve of his male form.

"I want you," he moaned through ragged breaths. "And, I know you want me."

"No."

"You wouldn't respond as you do, if that was true," he reasoned kissing her throat. Randall swept her into his arms and carried her upstairs. After lowering her to her feet, he walked over to turn down the bed.

"I want our first time to be slow and fulfilling," Randall managed. His lips moved over hers; his hands exploring, caressing and urging her closer.

"You are like a newly discovered intoxicating sensation, Lisa. Touch me," he encouraged.

She unbuttoned his shirt as her hands slipped inside to feel the sinewy muscles. He moaned deep in his throat. Closing his eyes, Randall cupped her derriere. Clothing was scattered randomly across the floor. He cradled Lisa's knees with one arm and gently laid her on the bed while he lowered himself.

"Your hair is like silk, and your skin like Dresden."

Longingly, she sighed as her arms encircled his neck. His lips took possession of one rosy peak.

"Tell me how much you want me," he whispered softly.

"I want you Randall."

He gasped as Lisa's hand swept down his torso. He rolled atop her, kissing her hungrily. Breathing raggedly, he withdrew a few seconds later.

"Please don't tease me!" she cried as she arched her back.

Once again Randall took her into his arms. He taught Lisa to savor the moment and how to please him. They were no long on earth, but in the clouds, floating.

Satiated, he continued to hold Lisa. She had never experienced such volatile emotions. Lisa suspected once he achieved his goal, he would add her to the list of broken hearts.

Intertwined, they fell asleep.

Much later that night, they made love a second time. This time it was slower.

"Why didn't you tell me?" he questioned.

"Does it matter?"

"Of course," he hesitated. "I hope I didn't hurt you."

"No. You were wonderful," Lisa reassured. "So gentle."

His heart swelled with pride. Brushing a dark wisp of hair from her face, Randall released a deep sigh. This woman elicited unfamiliar feelings.

The next few days passed rapidly to Lisa's regret. They spent time either on the beach playing cards and scrabble or sitting on the patio at sunset. Randall's shoulder was much better now, only a yellowish bruise remained. Tomorrow Lisa would return to Houston.

As she spent each day with Randall and slept in his arms at night, Lisa grew accustomed to his company. Frightened by the new emotions, Lisa suspected it would end. She was certain he had feelings for her although he never claimed he loved for her.

"What are your plans when you return to Houston?" Randall asked, sipping coffee at breakfast.

"I will take over the advertising firm."

"Good. I'd like to see more of you," he smiled. "It's great to be here. I can't remember when I've felt more at ease."

"I could stay here forever."

"We could go back together, if you like?" he suggested.

"Oh, really?"

"Yes, we can return both cars in Harlingen and go by plane."

"We can stay a day longer," she agreed.

"Now that's settled, let me take you to dinner? It would be nice to dress up for one night while we're here."

"I thought you'd never ask."

~****~

**CHAPTER 4**

Dinner proved to be a success. The seafood was tasty. Just the same, Lisa considered the company better by far as they drove back. Gazing at the stars that night, they sat in silence.

"What will you do when we return, Randall?"

"The usual, return to work. Spend time with my father."

"What about Clarissa? Surely your father hopes you will marry?"

"Everyone assumes," he paused. "Although it's quite impossible. I'm not the marrying kind."

To mask her disappointment, Lisa continued, "Surely one day you want to have a family of your own?"

"I don't really feel the need for it," he said flatly. His eyes became shuttered. It was as though a dark mask fell into place.

"How can you say that? Don't you want a son to carry on your name?"

If his childhood was any indication of the kind of life a child would experience, there was no contest, Randall considered. "Absolutely not. I refuse to bring a child into this world. Life is complicated enough without being the cause of unhappiness."

His words sounded final. Inside, Lisa felt sick when she realized Randall had taken advantage of her. He doesn't have a compassionate bone in his body! He's a selfish rake. *Foolish girl!* She couldn't wait to leave.

~****~

"Miss Stewart, please cancel my afternoon appointments. I have to finish the work on the Ferguson account," Lisa said as she thumbed through several papers on her desk. This was one of Franklin Advertising's larger accounts and Lisa wanted to be sure all details were addressed.

"Yes, Miss Franklin."

A month had passed since the trip to Padre Island. Lisa had not heard a word from Randall. *What a colossal fool!* Convinced Randall rejected her she buried herself in her work. Steven had been patient while she learned the business. He always offered constructive criticism. Although Louise had not asked about the trip to Padre, Lisa suspected she knew.

"It's Friday. Let's celebrate your one month anniversary with the company. I'll take you to dinner," Steven suggested cheerfully as he walked into Lisa's office. "We could tie up loose ends on the William's account. What do you say?"

"Sounds great. What time?"

"I'll pick you up at seven."

Staring out the window, Lisa had trouble focusing on her work. She was tired most of the time. Perhaps she had a twenty-four hour bug? Stop driving yourself so hard. *He's not worth it.*

That night, Steven arrived on schedule. He helped her into the Acura and closed the door. "I thought we'd try some Italian food," he remarked. "If that suits you?"

"I love Italian," Lisa said with a smile.

Steven ordered eggplant parmigiana, and Lisa ordered the Lasagna. A short time later, the food arrived piping hot and it was excellent. After dinner, they had drinks and danced at a local night spot.

"You're a million miles away," he scolded softly. "What's on your mind?"

"I'm a little run down," Lisa reassured. "I'm glad you suggested going out."

"Let's dance?"

"I'd love to."

Steven held Lisa close as they danced to a slow tune. "Lisa, I'm attracted to you. I have been from the moment I saw you," he murmured close to her ear.

Thrown aback, Lisa lost a step. "What a sweet thing to say. We barely know one another."

"That's easily remedied," Steven challenged. "How do you feel about me?"

"I think you're handsome and debonair. You dance very well," she evaded, attempting to lighten the subject.

"Seriously. Wouldn't you like to know me better?"

"You're a wonderful person, Steven, but I'm not sure that's a good idea," Lisa began. "We work together. Eventually it would lead to problems. You understand?"

"No. I'm sorry I don't," Steven replied. "I've learned a little about you. We enjoy many of the same things – concerts, plays and our work.

"That's true," she agreed. "And, I do love your company."

"No problem," he drawled as he ushered Lisa to their table.

"What do you like to do in your spare time?" Lisa questioned.

"I enjoy the Museum of Natural History and concerts at Jones Hall," Steven responded. "The Alley Theatre performs hit Broadway plays."

"I'd like to see the museum, that sounds interesting," Lisa said.

"How's Saturday?"

"Could we?"

"I'll pick you up at eleven, then we'll go to lunch," Steven offered, a twinkle in his eyes.

They arrived at the Martin home at midnight. Steven walked Lisa to the door and he kissed her lightly, then departed.

Louise was seated in the parlor as Lisa entered the house. "Did you have a nice time dear?"

"Yes, thank you," Lisa replied from the doorway.

"Come and sit with me for awhile," Louise encouraged, patting the sofa with one hand. Lisa crossed the room.

"You don't look well, dear. Are you ill?" Louise queried.

"Just a little run down. I plan to slow down," Lisa answered, hugging her aunt.

"How's work coming?"

"I think things are going well. The clients seem content and Steven has been helpful."

"That's good to hear. I want you to be happy," Louise acknowledged. "Randall telephoned while you were out. I am afraid, I let it slip that you were with Steven. He sounded upset."

"I couldn't care less what Randall thinks. There's nothing to apologize for, you've been wonderful. My father has the best sister. You loved him very much."

"At times I can't believe Jeremy's gone," Louise said with tears in her eyes. Lisa moved closer and embraced the older woman, patting her aunt's back affectionately.

"You're grieving and I've thought only of myself. Can you forgive me?"

"Don't be silly. I'm glad you're here," Louise said as she withdrew. "I love you, too. You know," she laughed, "I remember Jeremy used to ride his tricycle buck-naked down the side walk."

"He did?"

"Our mother was sure the neighbors would never let us live it down. Funniest thing, the way the past comes to mind."

"Was he always a rascal?"

"Jeremy was a good kid. He just liked to try things."

"You have fond memories of your childhood," Lisa said quietly.

A short time later the women grew weary and retired for the night.

Lisa settled comfortably in bed. The telephone rang just as she pulled the covers to her shoulders. Who would call as such a late hour? Again the telephone rang.

"Hello?" Lisa inquired as she lifted the receiver.

"Lisa?" a voice questioned.

"Yes? This is Lisa."

"It's Randall. I apologize for calling late. I called earlier and you were out," he explained with emphasis on the last three words.

"I received your message," Lisa replied curtly. "Do you know what time it is Randall?"

"Yes. I —"

Before he could finish the statement, Lisa said brusquely, "What do you want?

"Lisa, I need to talk to you." His voice grew impatient.

She remained silent.

"I just returned from a business trip. I'd like to see you."

A wave of remembrance washed over her. Her hormones had no sense of propriety! Lisa's pulse coursed rapidly though her veins. A part of her recalled his absence over the last month. She could feel the heat rise in her cheeks. Would she allow him to pop in and out of her life at will? If she allowed this, could she live with a lowered self-esteem? Lisa knew women who became involved with self-centered men were destined for heartbreak. Lisa found the thought distasteful.

She drew a deep breath and to her surprise, her voice was bland. "Oh, really?"

Even as she spoke her subconscious cried, "But he's the most exciting man you've ever met. Lisa shook herself mentally. This called for a cool, calm reserve she reminded herself miserably.

Summoning all of her self-control, Lisa struggled to keep her voice steady. "Randall, I'm sure your business is demanding. Why is it so important to see me, now?"

"I would think that's obvious."

Silence prevailed.

"I know what you must be thinking, but I can explain," Randall began. "Have dinner with me?"

"Why should I?"

"You're angry."

"No. Disappointed."

"C'mon Lisa, let me explain. Have dinner with me?"

"It's twelve thirty, and we're both tired. We're incompatible. Let's just leave it that way."

"Fine. If that's the way you want it?"

"Yes. Goodnight, Randall."

Inside, Lisa trembled. It was one of the most difficult things she'd ever done. Giving Randall up, was for the best. *The man would break her heart*!

~****~

"Good morning Louise," Lisa greeted, taking a seat at the table.

"You look better. Sleeping late helped," Louise said peering above the newspaper. "And, laughter's good medicine."

"I feel better."

"What's on the agenda?"

"Steven's taking me to the Museum of Natural History."

"You'll enjoy it." Louise rose. Kissing Lisa's forehead, she said, "I've agreed to meet the girls for brunch. I have to run."

"Have fun." Lisa replied to her aunt's retreating figure.

Lisa found the Museum of Natural History displays impressive. They opted for lunch after the tour.

"I thought we'd try Butera's," Steven offered. "It's a delicatessen."

"Great. I'm starved." A broad smile covered her face.

"It's good to see you smile again," Steven added. His gaze shifting to her mouth. He squeezed her hand.

"You make me feel good."

"That's a start," he answered steering the car into an available parking space. " I gather, you enjoyed the museum?" Steven grinned.

"It was informative." Lisa beamed.

"May I help you?" a young man asked from behind the counter at Butera's.

"Yes. I'll have the Quiche Lorraine and iced tea, " Lisa said smoothly as she moved in the line, her gaze scanning the different salads and desserts on display.

"And you, sir?"

"I'll have a tuna sandwich on whole wheat and a Perrier," Steven replied. Well into the meal, Steven mused, "You're like a child in a candy store."

"Thank you, I think," Lisa commented with an impish grin.

Steven drove around Memorial Park and pointed out sites of interest. Lisa thought the dense forest of Memorial Park had the most unique jogging trail. It was covered with wood shavings with several joggers present.

~****~

"Good morning, Miss Franklin," Miss Stewart greeted. "They're waiting in your office."

"Hello Kim," Lisa said as she approached her secretary's desk. "Who's waiting?"

"Mr. Alexander and Mr. Barryman."

What a way to start the morning, Lisa considered -- a confrontation. What could Randall possibly want?

"Morning, Lisa," Steven commented as she entered her office.

"Hello, Steven. Randall." Lisa greeted with bravado. "What can I do for you?"

"Barryman wants to hire us to do some advertising promotions for his firm," Steven remarked.

Randall inclined his head. "How are you, Lisa?"

Why did he choose us? Lisa wondered. She could do without the whole scenario.

"Fine, thank you. And you?" Lisa managed, striding past Randall. A maelstrom of emotions overcame her. Her eyes narrowed, and she inhaled deeply before placing her briefcase on the floor. Lisa forced a smile.

"What's on your mind?" Lisa said with saccharine sweetness, her fingers interlaced on the desk top.

"I have several new malls and hotels I'd like to promote. Some are finished, others are not. In some areas, the malls will provide the only shopping for consumers. I want to attract the right kind of businesses," Randall explained.

"I see," she said dryly.

"I have a few ideas," Randall added, through shuddered eyes. He was like a stranger.

"How is it, that you considered us, for such a large project?" Lisa questioned.

"Everyone knows, Franklin Advertising is the best," Randall replied, arching a brow. "I've outlined our needs to Steven. If you have no further questions, I really must go."

"Barryman, thank you for your confidence in us," Steven said. "We'll put together some ideas and we'll be in touch."

"Goodbye," Randall said, shaking Steven's hand. "Good day, Lisa."

What a *pompous arse*! This was a side of Randall Lisa found distasteful. The nerve! He marched in with such indifference and never offered to explain. The man's a robot.

"This calls for a celebration," Steven exclaimed. "I've tried to get him to return my calls for months. All of a sudden, it's in the bag."

"I wonder." Lisa moved her hand to her chin.

"Have dinner with me tonight?"

"That's the best offer I've had all day."

Later that evening, Lisa questioned, "Where are we going?"

"It's a surprise."

"This is a residential area."

"C'mon, we'll have a drink." Steven helped her from the car and closed the door.

After a quick glance around the house, she sighed.

"This is well done. Did you have a decorator come in?"

"I have two sisters." Steven laughed. "What'll you have?"

"A glass of red wine."

"Coming up."

"The house was built in the sixties – very California," Lisa said, taking a seat on the barstool.

"I like it."

"You never mentioned coming here."

"It offers more privacy than a restaurant." Steven handed Lisa her drink. "I charcoal the best steaks, if I say so myself. You don't mind? I thought it better than venturing the crowds."

"Not at all. This if fine."

Steven's home reflected a woman's taste. It was warm and inviting with a rock fireplace. The furniture was upholstered in royal blue, green and beige fabric. Walnut shelves lined an entire wall with several books. Outside was an engaging patio with a Japanese garden and fountain. A reflection of the owner Lisa thought. Everything was in its place.

"Great. I propose a toast," Steven added, lifting his glass to Lisa's. "Here's to good business, good health and friendship!"

"Salud!"

"I'm glad you could join me for dinner," he murmured, leaning to kiss her neck.

"My pleasure."

He rose. "I'll put the steaks on. Relax. I'll be right back."

"Can I help?"

"You're a guest. Everything's ready except the steak and potatoes."

She glanced around the room, then her eyes fixed on the stereo. Lisa rose. She scanned the audio compact discs. Evidently, he liked jazz and classical music. Ah, Shirley Horne! Pushing the audio compact disc into the stereo, she listened. This is heaven! she thought arranging herself on the sofa. Eyes closed, Lisa felt something wet and furry. Suddenly, her eyes flew open. A brown and white Springer spaniel licked her ankles.

"Who are you?" Lisa cooed, stroking the dog's head and back.

"I see you've met Schultze," Steven said from the hallway.

"Yes, she's loveable."

"Like her owner," he challenged.

"No doubt," she laughed as Schultze climbed into her lap.

"She approves of my taste in women."

Steven was dressed in jeans that clung to his long thighs and a blue Madre shirt. His rangy athletic carriage was agile as he approached her side. Damn! He was gorgeous -- definitely male. Why hadn't she noticed before?

"Feeling better?" he drawled.

"Yes. You certainly know how to live."

Hugging Schultze's neck, Steven replied, "We aim to please."

~****~

CHAPTER 5

The Springer spaniel jumped from Lisa's lap. Steven moved closer, draping an arm around her.

The dog began to bark.

"I smell smoke. You'd better check the steaks," Lisa warned.

"Oh, damn!" Steven growled as he bolted. On the patio, he snapped at the dog, "killjoy!"

He muttered an expletive under his breath. Lisa laughed.

As Steven returned to her side, he smiled. "Luckily, we caught the steaks just in time. It won't be long, now."

"Will you help me set the table?" he asked."Lisa, will you get the candles?"

During dinner Steven asked, "How's your steak?"

"Excellent," Lisa said with approval."Tell me about yourself."

"I'm the youngest of five children – two brothers and two sisters. I have great parents, not much money but lots of love in my family."

"I saw football trophies on the mantel. You never mentioned you played."

"In high school and college, I received a football scholarship. I was good or so they say," Steven commented.

"Your life is laid out. Have you always known what you want?" Lisa asked thoughtfully.

"Scarcely. I worked part-time and played football to pay for my education. It hasn't been easy, but then nothing worthwhile ever is."

"I find we have more in common all the time," Lisa said more to herself.

Candlelight bathed the room in a gentle glow as jazz bellowed from the stereo. After dinner, they moved into the living room.

"Your turn. Tell me what makes you tick?" Steven prodded.

"You really want to know?"

"Absolutely, or I wouldn't have asked."

"Unlike you, I remember my parents didn't get along. My father was ambitious. We didn't have much money. My mother encouraged him to finish school. She put him through college. They fought until he finally divorced my mother for a young legal secretary," Lisa said solemnly.

"You don't have to talk about it," Steven whispered.

"I want to. I remember as if it were yesterday. I watched my mother turn from a beautiful, loving woman into a bitter cynic. He used her. After the divorce, it was as though she lost all purpose. She became obsessed with his betrayal. I think she hated him even when she died five years later. Funny how it affects you," Lisa said, a transfixed expression on her face.

Tears formed in her eyes that fell with increased frequency. Steven gathered her close.

"There, there now. Maybe crying is what you need. I should know," he cajoled. He kissed her temple and cheeks as though soothing a child.

"I'm sorry. You must think, I'm a cry baby." Lisa sobbed.

"Everyone has experiences they wish they had handled differently."

Lisa sniffled, it was as though a dam broke.

"You think, I'm so perfect? That couldn't be farther from the truth. Before leaving for college, I was involved with a high school sweetheart, Tracie. She became pregnant and wanted to marry me. I was just a scared, ambitious kid. I refused. Later I learned she fell down some stairs. There were complications and later, she died."

"I'm sorry, Steven."

"I blame myself for what happened to Tracie. I should've married her," he confessed. "I will never run away from responsibilities again."

"That's awful."

"I wanted you to know. Everyone experiences sorrow and joy, has hopes and dreams. That's what keeps us going. Hopefully we learn from our mistakes."

"Thank you, Steven."

Steven's head dipped. The kiss was filled with mixed emotions. Lisa clung to him.

"I haven't made time for a woman in my life. But this has changed. Just the same, I won't take advantage of your vulnerable state. But I warn you of my intentions."

"I appreciate your honesty," she replied.

"C'mon I'll take you home."

~****~

After breakfast, Randall entered his father's room. "Dad, I'm going to play racquetball at the club. Can I bring you anything?"

"Yes, a shapely blonde," Daniel joked.

"You must be feeling better," Randall answered. "Are you sure you'll be alright?"

"Of course, son. Go and have a good time," Daniel encouraged. "I'll give Mrs. Peterson a bad time."

"The number for the club is on your bedside table," Randall added. "Call if you need anything."

The green Ferrari roared to life and Randall pulled from the driveway into traffic.

He arrived at the racquet club and waited until a room was available, then moved his things inside. After several minutes, he wiped the sweat from his brow with a forearm. He was aggressive today, slamming the ball mercilessly against the wall.

Racquetball would cool the aggression that simmered just below the surface. Repeatedly he slammed the ball. Each time it returned for punishment. Would he never feel at ease? He had it all – power, money, and position. Women chased him incessantly. Why was there a roaring inferno inside that threatened to consume him? Randall wondered.

At last he grew weary. He'd do a few laps around the pool, it will help cool the fire. After five laps of the Olympic pool, Randall climbed out and dried himself with a towel.

"Randall, Randall," a female voice beckoned.

Searching the room, his gaze centered on Clarissa dressed in a short tennis frock. She waved. He ambled toward her.

What the hell! She's crazy about me. Go with the flow, he thought.

"Hello wet, wild and handsome," Clarissa purred.

"Clarissa." He inclined his head."What's up?"

"Jenny and I just finished a few rounds of tennis. Will you join us in something tall and cool?" Clarissa invited.

"Sure. I'll meet you in the restaurant after I change," he replied, smiling.

Damn! He needed female companionship. He had been moody of late that everyone accused him of being a tyrant. *Find the handle, buddy!*

Seated across from Clarissa in the restaurant, Randall shifted his gaze to the waitress approaching.

"What'll you have?" the young woman asked, poised with an order pad in hand.

"Perrier," Randall answered.

"I'll have the same," Clarissa added.

The waitress returned moments later with their drinks and departed.

"Where's Jenny?" he questioned, sipping his drink.

"She had to leave. Said she had some errands. I haven't seen much of you lately, Randall. Where have you been?" Clarissa remarked.

"Lately I've had to travel for contract negotiations and project related problems. You name it," Randall replied. "I need to unwind."

"Poor thing. I know what you need," Clarissa said provocatively. "A good massage to release the tension."

"You volunteering?"

"I might be persuaded," Clarissa teased. "But it's going to cost you."

"Pray tell?"

"Dinner," she said flatly.

"I can handle that," Randall uttered. "How's Aaron?"

"He's fine. You should follow his example," Clarissa scolded. "My brother and his new wife are very happy."

"Married? When did this happen?"

"Recently. Unlike you, he grew up with scruples," Clarissa explained. "He's responsible now and has a good job."

"I don't believe it," Randall commented. "My childhood confidante – married. We were such rebels."

"The pranks the two of you played on the neighbors," Clarissa began. "You should be ashamed."

"I suppose you're right," he said blandly.

Old memories reminded Randall of the differences between he and Aaron. It was hard to believe five years had passed since their last meeting. Aaron was steady and always knew what he wanted out of life. Whereas Randall's driving force was in pursuit of his parent's attention and approval. Their time together was brief, just the same Randall looked up to Aaron like an older brother. Growing up, Clarissa spent her time trying to gain Randall's attention. He recalled the times she had tried to be one of the boys just to be near Randall. And he was mindful of their first date.

"Randall? You have a faraway look." Clarissa interrupted his reverie.

"What?"

"When will you call for me?"

"Eight o'clock. Wear something pretty."

"You're awful," Clarissa scolded mockingly.

"I'll see you tonight," he remarked absently, as he rose from the chair.

As she observed his departing figure, she said to herself, "Thank heaven."

~****~

"Ready?" Randall asked as Clarissa opened her door.

"One moment. I'll get my wrap."

"As always, you're a sight to behold." Randall released a wolf whistle, as his gaze travelled her length.

"Where are you taking me?"

"I thought we would dine French tonight?"

"Superb."

The maitre d' directed the couple to a cozy table in a dimly lit corner surrounded by plants.

"I'll have a scotch and water," Randall ordered. "The lady will have a vodka tonic."

"Oui, messier," the maitre d' responded. "Right away."

Minutes later, the waiter arrived with the drinks. Randall proceeded to order for them.

"How's Daniel?" Clarissa asked sweetly.

"He has good and bad days."

"That's too bad," Clarissa replied. "It's quite a responsibility to shoulder."

"I manage."

Clarissa could not imagine why he was evasive. Well, she would have to guide the conversation in the direction she wanted it to go.

"You know there's a silly rumor going around that you were with Lisa in Padre," Clarissa laughed. "And that you're interested in her."

Randall hedged. "Who would start such nonsense or believe it for that matter?"

"I knew it," Clarissa said. "The minute I heard it." Randall shifted his gaze to look around the room. "Also, I understand Franklin Advertising has gone downhill."

With Clarissa's statement his gaze focused on her, his eyes narrowed. "That's a damn lie!" he growled.

"Keep your voice down," Clarissa chided. "All I know, the word is, that their clients are dissatisfied."

"You heard wrong."

Puzzled, Clarissa forged ahead, "I was working on a new account the other day and I overheard an interesting rumor. It seems, Lisa has been involved with Steven as well. Need I say more?"

"You've said enough already," Randall said through clenched teeth.

"They have been seen together around town," Clarissa supplied enthusiastically.

The waiter arrived at that moment with the chateaubriand. The food although beautifully served was tasteless to Clarissa as she kept a watchful eye on Randall. He was preoccupied tonight. He ordered another round of drinks after the meal. Clarissa moved closer to him.

Randall forced a smile and moved an arm around Clarissa, as she stroked his thigh with one hand. "Let's go to your place," Randall suggested.

"You sure?" Clarissa inquired with a playful grin, rubbing his lower leg with her foot.

"C'mon, let's go," he whispered. "Or I won't be responsible for what happens."

"Sure baby," she cooed.

Randall dropped some bills on the table and they left the restaurant.

You blew it with Lisa. She's seeing Steven. *Damn!* Who cares? Randall reasoned. He tried to explain, but Lisa would not listen. Forget her. Any man would give his soul for Clarissa's undivided attention. *So give it!*

Clarissa sensed Randall's tension. She would help him relax, she thought. He stole my heart years ago – *he's mine.*

~****~

**CHAPTER 6**

Monday, Steven walked into Lisa's office with some folders in hand. "Let's go out for lunch?" Steven suggested as he glanced at his watch. "I'll treat."

"How can I refuse?" Lisa smiled.

Steven lightly held Lisa's elbow as he ushered her into the restaurant. They almost collided with Randall and Clarissa. Lisa wanted to melt into the carpet.

"Hello Lisa," Randall said sardonically. "Steven." He gave a polite nod.

"How are you and Clarissa?" Lisa asked with feigned interest.

"Couldn't be better," he said sarcastically. Clarissa clung possessively to his arm.

"You're looking well, Barryman," Steven remarked, wryly. "Will you join us for lunch?"

Lisa could not believe the conversation. Surely Randall would want Clarissa to himself. *He has his bloody nerve!*

Randall graciously accepted the invitation without a glance in Clarissa's direction. They were shown to a table for four. Why had she agreed to lunch with Steven? Lisa did not want to sit at the same table with Randall and Miss Perfect.

A waiter approached the table. "May I bring you something to drink while you decide?"

"I'll have a Perrier," Randall supplied as he looked venomously at Lisa. His eyes blazed fire.

"A diet coke for me," Clarissa ordered graciously.

"What will you have, Lisa?" Steven asked.

"A glass of iced tea with lemon, please," Lisa stated as she turned to Steven, smiling.

"I'll have the same," Steven requested.

"I've missed seeing you," Clarissa said haughtily as she glanced in Lisa's direction. "Your work must be very demanding, Lisa. How do you find Houston?"

"It can be demanding," Lisa conceded. "I think Houston is just the place I'd like to call home. Steven has been wonderful and my aunt is truly a dear. How's the decorating business?"

"It's all or nothing, but I enjoy my work. Randall is such good company, filling in and helping whenever needed. I would be lost without him," Clarissa said as she gazed adoringly at him. "We've been inseparable. Isn't that right dear?"

"Lisa and I have enjoyed one another's company, too," Steven interrupted unexpectedly, grasping her hand in his on the table.

Randall looked as though he just sat on a tack and had no wish to create a scene.

"Lisa, that is an interesting dress you're wearing," Clarissa said with feigned interest. "I know the name of the best couturier, do let me give you his name. I'm sure he can help you find something. In California the dress is more casual, but here, do let me help you."

What a snob, Lisa thought. She wanted to lash back, but refrained. Instead, she replied sweetly, "Thank you, Clarissa. I would appreciate that."

Undeterred by Lisa's comment, Clarissa continued. "Randall and I attended the best play the other night at the Alley Theatre. We met one of your clients, Mr. Ferguson. A dear friend of mine. I decorated his office and home. You remember me telling you about it, Randall?"

"Yes, I do," Randall said as he peered suspiciously at Clarissa.

That did it! Lisa wanted to strangle her right here.

"It seems he's unhappy with your firm," Clarissa added. "He feels, he hasn't obtained the same results, since your father – the dear soul, passed away. Oh my, I've chattered on so, I do hope you'll forgive me?"

Lisa smoldered. Listen Clarissa, mind your own business, she wanted to say. Keeping her temper in check, Lisa answered, "I really appreciate you letting me know what Mr. Ferguson has expressed. It's our business to find out what his specific needs are."

Clarissa's smile failed to reach her eyes. Lisa did not miss the tension on Clarissa's face as her comment found it's mark.

Lunch was tasteless to Lisa. She was uncomfortable as Randall's eyes followed her every move. Why was he acting as though she was a traitor? Her palm itched to slap his face. Why did he accept the luncheon invitation? Her assessment was right on the money. He wanted to flaunt Clarissa in her face. Well, Clarissa was welcome to him. Together, they could take a flying leap, Lisa thought.

Lisa was relieved to leave the restaurant, she reflected as she drove home that evening. Steven rescued her and helped her save face at Clarissa's prodding.

Lisa took a seat in a large upholstered chair and settled back to relax. Just as she lifted a magazine, the telephone rang.

"Hello?" Lisa answered.

"How are you dear?" Louise beamed.

"Fine, Louise. How's Cancun?"

"The girls and I are having a time," Louise began. "The cruise has been wonderful. I met his awful little man. Well, I'll tell you about it later."

"Everything's fine here. We miss you." Lisa feigned happiness.

"Okay. What's wrong?" Louise demanded.

"I don't know what you mean?"

"Listen, you can't fool an old lady," Louise responded. "You forget, I've been there."

"That a fact?"

"Hasn't Randall called?"

No response followed.

"Don't play games with me, Lisa," Louise said impatiently.

"Oh, Louise," Lisa said, dismissing all pretense. "I've made a mess of my life! Trust a man and look where it leaves you!"

"Tell me about it," Louise encouraged.

"I've seen Randall a few times since Padre, he acts so callous. Men have no conscience. I was warned about him. I went against my better judgment. It's my own fault."

"You're not pregnant?"

"Nothing like that," Lisa said solemnly. "You knew all along. I've tried to forget him. I've even gone out with Steven."

"But it's not the same."

"Why do women always fall victim to his type?" Lisa sniffled.

"That's easy. They have a practiced line," Louise said, anger lacing her voice. "How are things with Steven?"

"He's in love. I enjoy him very much, but he doesn't make me feel the way Randall does."

"Damn Randall, anyway," Louse said waspishly. "The boy has always been a difficult one."

~****~

The next morning, Lisa thumbed through the papers on her desk.

"Miss Fran—"

Randall crashed through the door. Kim followed close at his heels.

"Miss Franklin, I tried," Kim said frantically.

"It's all right Kim. That will be all," Lisa said transferring her gaze to Randall. Kim closed the door behind her. "What's this all about?"

"I'm accustomed to having my calls returned," Randall growled. "Look, if you don't want the account. Say so!"

"You have your nerve! Who do you think you are?"

For a moment Randall blinked several times, took a breath and settled himself in a chair. Plowing a hand through his hair, Randall said, "What about the project proposals I was promised over a week ago?"

"Kim, bring me Mr. Barryman's file," Lisa requested over the intercom. She worked to gain her composure. "Would you care for coffee?"

"I take mine black," Randall muttered. "Steven said the proposals for the California project would be on my desk a week ago. I have deadlines to meet."

"I understand," she replied. "Steven was called out of town on another project. May I help you?"

Kim opened the door, "Here's the Barryman Corporation file. Will there be anything else, Miss Franklin?"

"Thank you, Kim," Lisa stated. "Coffee. Mr. Barryman will take his black." She opened the file. "Now, let's take a look."

Moments later, Kim returned with the coffee and left.

Randall rose and walked around the desk as he moved an arm to the back of her chair.

Startled, Lisa gasped and the chair tilted backward. Randall caught it. "Ah-h-h!" Lisa bellowed.

Repositioning the chair, he drew her tightly into his embrace. Trembling, Lisa clung to him. He rocked her in his arms.

"You all right?" he questioned softly. Their gazes locked.

Though she willed them, the words were not forthcoming. She bobbed her head slowly.

A distinct deep sigh was heard in the room. Whether she or Randall made it, Lisa could not say. Forget his motives, just be glad to be in his arms again. Randall's mouth plundered hers.

Several moments later, Randall raised his head. Lisa was mute. Caught in the moment, she returned his kiss with equal fervor.

"Oh Lisa," Randall said, brushing his lips along the nape of her neck.

Regaining her composure, she pulled back slightly. "What are we doing? I must be mad."

"Enjoying each other," Randall supplied softly.

Preening herself, Lisa squared her shoulders. "Am I to feel honored that you have an opening in your schedule?" she questioned, trying not to sound breathless.

"You enjoyed it as much as I did," he said quietly. "Don't deny it. I'm not buying."

"I-I …"

"Don't ruin it Lisa. I've missed you," he encouraged.

Turning her back to him, Lisa said, "You think, you can pop in and out of my life at will." Her hands still trembling.

"I tried to explain. You wouldn't listen," Randall reasoned.

"It's too late," she snapped.

"I didn't plan what happened, but I don't regret it," he said calmly. "My purpose in coming here was business. You'll have to accompany me to California to get the information you'll need. We leave in two days."

"I'll be ready," she replied.

A twinkle in his eye, he winked. "Until then." He turned and departed.

Wouldn't you know it! He pops back into my life unexpectedly and my traitorous body is ready, and willing to forgive. Unbelievable! Why do I always say yes, when I mean no? An inner voice said because he makes you feel alive. Lisa couldn't deny the chemistry between them.

~****~

She has doubts, Randall considered. Can you blame her? You will have to win back her trust. Women like to be romanced, he mused.

"Mary, come into my office," Randall instructed his secretary. The door opened to his opulent office, Mary stepped inside.

"Yes, sir?"

"I want you to do something for me as soon as possible," Randall said with a sly grin.

~****~

"Good night, Miss Franklin," Kim said as she stuck her inside Lisa's door.

"Have a good evening. Thanks, Kim," Lisa commented looking up from her work.

"Oh, I almost forgot. Someone sent flowers – a roomful, in fact. Carnations and roses!" Kim exclaimed. "Here's a note."

"Why didn't you tell me?" Lisa mused. "Where?"

"They're in the waiting area. My desk is covered, too. Whatever he did, I would forgive him. Well, goodnight."

Rising from her desk, Lisa walked to the waiting room. "It's true! Who?"

Remember the note! Opening the envelope, she read:

Lisa, this is all new to me. Give us another chance. Have dinner with me tonight? Randall

At that moment the front door opened, Randall entered Franklin Advertising. "I see they were delivered," he said glancing around the room.

"Why didn't you rent a billboard?" Lisa scolded mockingly.

"I thought about it." He smiled.

"They're lovely. You should not trouble yourself," Lisa murmured.

"Does this mean, you'll have dinner with me?" Randall queried expectantly.

"Yes, I will."

"Lock up and we're out of here," he said, laughingly.

"I should have my head examined," she said in disbelief.

"We'll do that later. C'mon." He nudged her toward the door.

The emerald Ferrari's engine purred to life. Randall handled the automobile with finesse through the busy traffic. He slipped a disc into the stereo. Beethoven's Fifth Pastoral filled the air.

"Where are we going?"

"To the airport."

"What?"

"You agreed to have dinner with me," he reasoned.

"The airport wasn't what I expected."

"Benihana's in Los Angeles is great Japanese," Randall chuckled, his gaze intent on Lisa.

"You sneak! I'm not prepared to go to California."

"You can pick up whatever you need in L.A.," he dismissed.

"But --"

He pulled the automobile into a multi-level parking area. Ushering her through the crowd, Randall directed her to a private gate.

"We're not supposed to enter," Lisa began. "The sign indicates-- "

"This way," Randall insisted.

"Good evening Mr. Barryman," the pilot greeted. "We'll depart in ten minutes."

Turning to Randall, Lisa said, "You're sure of yourself!"

Randall shrugged his shoulders. "Just hopeful."

Aboard the Lear jet, a steward greeted, "Good evening, folks. Would you care for cocktails?"

"What would you like?" Randall asked with a broad smile.

She shrugged her shoulders.

"We'll have an Espresso," Randall ordered. "It will relax you."

Effortlessly, the jet ascended into the air. Lisa's stomach dropped a notch. *This isn't happening!* she thought.

As if he could read her thoughts, Randall winked and squeezed her hand.

Two and half hours later, the plane landed at Los Angeles International. "Ladies and gentlemen the temperature is 57 degrees, it's a clear night in Los Angeles. Welcome and enjoy your stay," the pilot announced over the speaker system.

Unbuckling their seat belts, Randall and Lisa rose and exited the plane. A midnight blue limousine awaited. A chauffeur stood beside an open door.

"This is like a fairy tale," Lisa said in amazement.

"All for you." He laughed.

"I can't believe I'm in Los Angeles. You're full of surprises!" she added. "I'm not dressed to go out. You should have given more notice."

"Spontaneity brings added flavor to life," Randall supplied.

"We'll dine at Benihana's," Randall instructed the chauffeur.

"Very good, sir."

Benihana's was elaborate with red paper lanterns, and oriental artwork. A small Japanese woman greeted them, then she proceeded to escort them to a table.

"The chefs are trained in Hong Kong especially for Benihana's. The food is prepared at your table," Randall said. "I think you'll enjoy it."

"I know," Lisa agreed. "They are skilled with knives. I always wonder, what if they miss?"

"You've eaten here?" Randall inquired. "Of course, you're from L.A."

"No problem. I love it."

Lisa watched in fascination as the chef prepared the food with skillful expertise.

"I'm glad you came with me," Randall said as they completed the meal.

"This has been an unusual day," Lisa replied. "Totally unexpected, but--"

"But what?"

"Louise must wonder where I am," she responded. "You didn't give me a chance."

"To say no?" he finished. "We should leave for the hotel. You can call from there."

"I will."

"Check, please." Randall requested as the waiter passed.

He dropped a sizeable tip on the table and guided Lisa from the restaurant.

After arriving at the hotel, he opened her door then handed Lisa the card. Studying her for a moment, he lingered as though collecting his thoughts.

"It's been a long day. Get some rest. I'll see you in the morning," Randall said, his eyes searching hers.

"Thank you for the memorable evening," Lisa managed. "Good night." She hoped he couldn't read her confusion. Abruptly, he turned on his heel and left.

The suite was enormous befitting a queen, Lisa thought. She noted a huge bed, ceiling to floor drapes that covered a large set of sliding glass doors with a spectacular view of the city.

The velvety night appeared lit by fireflies in the distance – Los Angeles. Life was strange. Truly, one never knows what treasures life may offer. Take the gifts life offers and never, take it all, too seriously. These were the lessons life taught her.

After a warm bath, Lisa rested comfortably in the canopied bed against several pillows. She couldn't believe she was with Randall. Steven's out of town. *Someone had to do it!* That sounded shallow even to her.

Lisa's thoughts moved to Randall. He's a rogue – pure and simple. If you remember this, and you'll be fine she told herself.

Things were going well, Randall considered as he unfastened his tie and rolled up his sleeves. Lisa's here and Randall was relieved he had the foresight to leave earlier. He might have rushed her -- frightened her. Take it slow, he chided himself. He wanted her like no other woman. Randall wanted her in his bed at least until he got her out of his system.

Tomorrow was Wednesday and it would be a long day. He would take Lisa to the project site and begin the preliminary work. It was late he considered, he should get some sleep.

The following day, Lisa took time dressing over a leisurely cup of coffee.

A knock at the door caught her attention. Randall stood lazily against the door frame, his legs crossed at the ankles as Lisa opened the door.

"Hello, Lisa. May I come in ?"

"Yes, please." She stepped aside.

"How's the room? Comfortable?"

"It's great. Thank you," Lisa commented.

"I hate to say it, but duty calls."

"Give me just a minute."

Randall helped Lisa into the rented Mercedes. Lisa thought they were leaving the area entirely, when he drove on and on. Finally, he pulled off the road into a large construction site.

"You never mentioned it was so big," Lisa remarked in amazement.

"Las Palmas is a complete community. Suburbia, if you will. It offers a country club with tennis, swimming, and golf. In addition, there is a shopping center, library, and professional buildings. Literally everything you need," Randall announced proudly. "This is my pet project."

"Amazing," Lisa uttered. "I cannot believe it!"

"I wanted you to see it in person," Randall confessed, waiting for a response. "What do you think?"

"I love it. I had no idea. You never let on about the caliber of this project.

"I think you can handle it."

"I appreciate your confidence. I won't let you down."

Randall's rich baritone laughter filled the air. "C'mon, I'll introduce you to Bruce, our architect," he said, opening the door for Lisa. He could see the excitement and challenge the project presented on her lovely face.

"I'll want to take several pictures. Do some research," Lisa rattled off. She paused to gather her thoughts.

"Whatever you need. Let me know," he remarked. A mischievous grin on his face.

Introductions were made and Randall was called away to handle problems on the project. Bruce gave Lisa a tour of the project.

"Have you known Mr. Barryman long?" Bruce asked casually.

"No, only a short time," Lisa replied. "Why do you ask?"

"I just wondered, why the change. The people who usually handle our advertising well, it's none of my business."

"Mr. Barryman has outdone himself this time," Lisa supplied approvingly. "I'm sure you'll be proud when it's completed."

"We're excited about it," Bruce conceded.
Two hours later, Bruce drove Lisa back to the construction office. When they arrived, Randall was in a heated discussion over the telephone.

"I don't care what your delivery problems are, Mitch. Sounds like a personal problem. Deliver by Friday or the deal's off," Randall demanded.

"It was nice meeting you, Lisa," Bruce said quietly. "The boss will handle the rest. I've an appointment."

"Thank you, Bruce. Bye."

~****~

**CHAPTER 7**

The receiver landed with a thud in its cradle as Randall released it. Heaving a deep sigh, he narrowed his eyes.

"Something wrong?" Lisa questioned demurely.

"Don't ask!" Randall barked.

"You don't have to shout," she countered.

"What?" he inquired incredulously.

"Speak to me in a civil tone or I'm leaving," Lisa demanded icily, turning her back to him. "I don't have to put up with this!"

"Okay, okay," Randall said, his tone lowered to an acceptable volume.

"If you think you can order me around," Lisa blurted. "Well, you are mistaken."

"Calm down," he said quietly.

"You owe me an apology," she snapped.

Randall blinked in amazement.

"You heard me," Lisa supplied, her hands planted firmly on her hips. "I'm not in the habit of being yelled at."

"You're a victim of bad timing."

"Randall are you sure you want me for the job? We're not hitting it off."

"I've signed a contract and I will honor it," he said under his breath.

"If that's the reason, I will be happy to let you off the hook. Hire someone more to your liking." She crossed over to the telephone.

"Lisa, wait!" Randall said, moving in her direction.

Extending a hand to halt his speech, Lisa lifted the telephone receiver and said, "I need a taxi, please. I'm located at --"

Randall took the phone from her and cradled it. His face was scarlet, his eyes blazed white heat. "I brought you here. I'll take you back," he said, his anger barely leashed.

"You can send me back to Houston," Lisa said pugnaciously.

He ploughed a hand through his hair, heaved a deep sigh and blinked several times. Lisa knew Randall was not accustomed to anyone disagreeing with him. He was at loss for words.

"Lisa, this has gotten out of hand. I'll take you back to the hotel." His face devoid of emotion. Once again, the stranger emerged.

The return trip was in silence. *He's a bully. Well, not with me!* Randall escorted her back to her hotel room and opened the door. Politely he excused himself and departed.

Watch your temper Barryman, he chided. Why did he lose control around Lisa? Usually he was self-assured and in control. *Hormones are dictating your life, get a grip!*

Why had she allowed herself to become involved in this situation? She would leave tomorrow. No, a small voice announced. Handle this like any other account. Leave after a job well done. *That is the answer!*

Thursday and Friday passed uneventfully. Randall was conveniently busy with decisions on the project. This left Lisa to perform her job in peace. Bruce answered Lisa's questions and directed her to resources to resolve problems.

After this trip, she would return to Houston and never see Randall again. Suddenly she remembered the way her mother gave into her father's fits of temper. She loathed women who were weak of character. *This is one woman who will not cower!*

Lisa was relieved her work was complete on Friday. A shower would relax her. Drying her damp hair, Lisa stepped from the shower. She thought she heard a knock at the door. Was her imagination playing tricks? The knocking persisted. She wrapped a towel around her head and slipped into a robe.

"Yes?" Lisa questioned. "Who is it?"

"Randall. May I come in?"

"Go away!"

"Five minutes is all I ask. Open the door, Lisa."

She hesitated.

"People are beginning to collect outside the door, Lisa. Are you going to open the door, or do I kick it down?"

"Alright!" Lisa said dryly. She stepped aside to allow Randall entry.

"Okay, let's have it!" Lisa demanded.

"Tisk, tisk, no manners," Randall scolded.

"This isn't funny, Randall."

He walked leisurely into the living room and settled himself on the sofa.

"I have to change. I wasn't expecting company," she said wryly.

"Don't change on my account."

"What do you want? Another round perhaps?"

"This --" he said as he approached, his lips claimed hers.

Lisa was dizzy and her knees weak. Of their own volition, her arms encircled his neck.

"Randall," Lisa whispered as she stepped back. "Why do you keep coming onto me? We're incompatible and you know it."

"We got off on the wrong foot. I don't know where this will lead, but Lisa I am drawn to you," he confessed. "Let's give it a chance?

"We've been through this before," Lisa admonished. "What do you take me for?"

"Let's back up a little," he cajoled. His words were tender as a caress. "It's more than a physical attraction, although I admit I want to take you to bed. I've never wanted a woman like this."

"You're resourceful. You'll find someone to accommodate you," Lisa said brusquely.

"If I wanted someone to accommodate me, it wouldn't be difficult."

"Why tell me?" Lisa yelled.

"You're the woman I want," he whispered, a sheepish grin on his face.

"Get out!"

"Be reasonable, Lisa."

"You weren't concerned when we returned from Padre. Why is it so bloody important now," she demanded.

"I've made mistakes," Randall confessed ruefully. "I want to make it up to you, Lisa. You're free to make a decision."

Lisa whirled to face Randall, but the room was empty. The only sound was the door as it closed silently behind him.

~****~

What was that awful noise? The ringing persisted. Bleary-eyed, Lisa searched for the telephone.

"Yes?" she questioned.

"Lisa? Is that you?" a voice asked.

"Yes. Hello, Steven," she greeted happily. "How are you?"

"Fine. I finished the Blakely account. How's it going in California?"

"I'm leaving for Houston this afternoon."

"Good. I've missed you," Steven's voice almost sang over the wire. "When will you arrive? I'll pick you up?"

"Seven-thirty."

"See you then." He rang off.

Lisa prepared her things for departure. Randall was unaware she planned to leave without him. She had had enough. It would be less painful this way.

The 747 glided into Hobby Airport like a lazy bird. Lisa knew she was in Houston when the sultry heat slapped her in the face as she stepped off the plane. She could see a large crowd gathered below. Hurriedly she checked the crowd for Steven.

"Here, Lisa!" Steven shouted above the noise, his arm waving in the air.

"It's good to see you," Lisa said gleefully.

"How did it go in California?"

"I think we have what we need for the job. The remainder can be handled over the telephone," Lisa replied.

"That's good news," Steven added. "I'll get the rest of your bags and we'll leave."

"This is all I brought with me."

"Most women would've taken everything they own. One bag, huh?" Steven said as he grasped the travel bag from her. Lisa smiled.

~****~

Moody, Randall bumped around the hotel room trying to figure out what went wrong. A second cup of coffee would certainly put matters into perspective. Why did he always lose his temper with Lisa? She could make him mad quicker that a colony of hornets.

Unable to sleep after the fracas with Lisa, he stayed up until dawn. Afterward he collapsed in bed and slept most of the day. It was four o'clock -- call her! He picked up the telephone, and punched out the numbers. The phone rang repeatedly.

~****~

The Acura moved easily through traffic.

"It's good to be home," Lisa said surprisingly. "I never thought I'd miss this place, but I have. They say Texas has a way of creating loyalty within its people. Guess I'm a Texan at heart?"

"I'm sure you are. In any event, I'm glad you're back," Steven drawled.

Lisa telephoned Louise on Wednesday to explain what happened. To Lisa's amazement, Louise took the news in stride. Didn't anything ever rattle her? Maybe it was the years of marriage to a cardiologist. Doctors left at the drop of a hat. Louise was accustomed to it.

The car swerved.

"Watch it fella!" Steven growled at a passing driver.

It was eight-thirty, and Saturday passed too quickly. The automobile stopped in front of the Martin home. Assisting Lisa from the car, Steven accompanied her inside.

"I know you're exhausted. Why don't you have a bath and change?" Steven suggested.

"Sounds good. What about you?"

"Is that an invitation to join you?" Steven teased, his brows moved upward.

"Absolutely not," Lisa responded as she began ascent of the stairs.

"I was afraid of that," Steven began. "I'll rustle up something cool."

~****~

Lisa clad in lounging pajamas, joined Steven in the living room. "Where is everyone?" she commented.

"Louise is at the opera tonight. She said she'd see you at breakfast. We have the place to ourselves," Steven replied.

"Really?"

"I didn't mean it, the way it sounds," Steven commented passing Lisa a glass of iced tea. "I have something to discuss with you."

"Everything alright at work?" Lisa asked, sipping her tea.

"Of course," he reassured. "My sister, Marnie, is getting married. My family is planning a shin-dig in Austin."

"That's wonderful. I'm happy for her."

"Yeah," he muttered arranging himself next to her on the sofa. His lips grazed her cheek. "Go with me Lisa?"

"I just returned from California, Steven," she hedged. "Who will manage the firm if we both go?"

"It's not until the weekend. We can finish up on Thursday. Then we can leave instructions for Kim and fly to Austin."

"I don't know."

"You will love Marnie. This is a special time for me, Lisa," Steven reasoned. "Share it with me?"

"When you put it that way, how can I refuse?"

"That was my intention," he chuckled.

"Why do I always agree to these things?" Lisa laughed.

"I'm just lucky, I guess." After finishing his drink, Steven said, "I'll call you tomorrow." He stood up.

Lisa followed his lead.

As quick as a heartbeat, Steven drew her close and his head dipped. Releasing her, he turned and crossed the room. The door closed behind him.

Are you sure you want to attend the wedding in Austin with Steven? she asked herself silently. Yes! Randall is an arrogant, self-serving womanizer. She knew the direction her life would take with him – heartbreak. Women who followed their hearts without considering the consequences, become a number. She could never settle for this. What do you want? an inner voice asked. Someone to love and to grow old with, children, a dog and a cat. What's wrong with that?

~****~

"How was California?" Louise asked at breakfast.

"I have what I need for this project," Lisa said flatly.

"That's it?" Louise said in disbelief. "I heard he sent you a roomful of flowers."

"Kim can't keep anything quiet!"

"Are you going to tell me about it?"

"He tricked me. I didn't know he meant California," Lisa defended.

Louise remained silent.

"Everything went well for awhile then he reverted to his loathsome self. We fought and I tried to back out of the deal," Lisa confessed.

"But it wasn't his idea, so he wouldn't hear of it," Louise supplied.

"How did you know?"

"A wild guess."

"I said some things I shouldn't have. It's better this way. He's an arrogant, self-serving mechanism!"

"You're in love with him!"

"Nothing happened in California," Lisa explained. "I never want to see Randall again, other than in business. This time, I'm ending it."

"This is worse than I thought," Louise said more to herself. "Have you considered a vacation?"

"I don't need a vacation. I can handle my own life."

"Of course, dear," Louise placated.

"Steven's sister is getting married this weekend. He asked me to go with him to Austin for the wedding. I accepted."

"A marvelous idea," Louise agreed. "You'll want to do some shopping."

"Yes. We plan to leave Thursday evening for Austin."

The women made plans for the week. After work, they would put a wardrobe together for Lisa. Louise considered if she kept Lisa busy, it would leave less time for her to fret over Randall. Time would take care of the rest.

~****~

**CHAPTER 8**

Randall arrived in Houston on Sunday afternoon. His purposeful stride demonstrated his ill mood. How could she leave without a word? So they had a disagreement? They said some ugly things. What did he expect?

He expected Lisa to be an adult. Chase after him like the rest. Hah! This was an example of the irresistible force meets the immoveable object. He was the force and Lisa, the object, he considered.

Randall drove like a man chased by a thousand demons. He would go home and check on his father and forget Lisa.

"Hello, son," Daniel Barryman greeted. "Glad you remembered where you live. I suppose, Mrs. Peterson's relieved, too. She won't have to put up with me any longer."

"Thanks Dad," Randall said, forcing his best smile. "It's good to be here."

"Join me in a glass of iced tea?" Daniel asked. "I was about to go out by the pool."

"Sure. Let me put my bag away. I'll be down in a few minutes.

Reluctant Heart

Daniel moved out to the patio by the pool.

~****~

Thursday arrived before Lisa realized it.

"Well that wraps it up," Steven said happily. "Did you leave a contact number with Kim in case she needs us?"

"Yes. I told her to call only if it was an emergency, otherwise it can wait until Monday," Lisa said with a sigh.

"Good," he murmured. "Ready?"

As they boarded the plane, Lisa nodded.

The plane landed in Austin thirty-five minutes later.

"Steven! Steven!" a male voice called over the crowd.

Steven scanned the large group. His gaze centered on his brother. He waved.

"Hey bubba," a tall dark-haired man said, embracing Steven.

"Curtis, I want you to meet--"

"Lisa," Curtis interrupted.

"How did you know my name?"

"You're all Steven talks about," Curtis answered, poking his fist playfully at Steven's waist.

"Curtis is my older brother," Steven explained.
"Mom's holding dinner. We'd better go," Curtis added.

The trip to the Alexander home was forty minutes from the airport. Austin was definitely the hill country. The streets went on forever, as well as the traffic.

79

Their home was nestled within a large group of trees just outside the main part of the city. Lisa would never have guessed that Steven grew up on a ranch.

The ranch was nice but nothing fancy, Lisa considered.

Curtis honked the horn announcing their arrival. An older woman and man stepped onto the porch.

"At last you're here," the woman exclaimed. "Son, how was your flight?"

"Good momma," Steven said embracing her. "It's good to see both of you."

"This is Lisa Franklin," Steven introduced, nudging her forward, his hand to the small of her back.

"Welcome to our home, Lisa," Mrs. Alexander said. "I've heard so much about you."

"Thank you," Lisa said shyly. "Did you know Steven was bringing someone with him?"

"Indeed. Come inside."

The men shook hands.

"You mentioned you were bringing a gal," Mr. Alexander teased. "But not such a pretty one."

"Dad!" Steven chided. "Don't give all my secrets away at once."

"Curtis and Tommy fetch their bags and bring them inside," Mrs. Alexander ordered.

"Sure, Ma." Both men left with the screen door slamming as it contacted the jamb.

"They never have learned not to slam the door," Mrs. Alexander said, shaking her head.

The four of them settled comfortably in the living room. The colonial furniture and wood burning fireplace lent a warmth to the Alexander home.

"Marnie and Bill will come by tomorrow. We've planned a rehearsal on Friday afternoon," Mrs. Alexander explained.

"Mom, we'd like to clean up," Steven said. "I'll show Lisa her room."

"She can use Marnie's old room. C'mon down for supper when you're finished."

Mrs. Alexander proved to be a good cook. The Alexanders were casual, friendly people, Lisa thought.

Much later that night standing outside Lisa's door, Steven said, "Thank you for coming."

"My pleasure. You have a nice family."

Lisa's bedroom reflected the same colonial decor as the rest of the house. The room was feminine with frilly curtains and bedspread. High school memorabilia covered the walls. Lisa bathed and prepared for bed. Nestled between the sheets, Lisa looked around the room. A tall hutch displayed dolls of various eras.

They were a close family, earthy and unpretentious. She envied Steven. He grew up with the security and love of a family to encourage him. This was something Lisa desperately desired. Her grandparents loved and encouraged her, but it was not the same as your parents. She wondered how life might have differed had they stayed together. Steven did not realize how fortunate he was.

The Alexander family shared their daily activities. They welcomed Lisa into their home and regarded her as one of the family. After dinner, everyone called an early night, she reflected. She learned this was routine day on the ranch.

"Good morning, Mrs. Alexander," Lisa said entering the kitchen the next morning.

"Morning, Lisa," Mrs. Alexander greeted. "Would you care for coffee, flap jacks and bacon?"

"Sounds fattening," Lisa teased. "Yes."

Mrs. Alexander poured a cup of coffee and passed it to her.

Lisa took a seat at the table. "Where's Steven? Everyone for that matter?"

"They left at six to tend the cattle. The flap jacks will be ready in a few minutes," Mrs. Alexander said, her eyes on the skillet.

"Why didn't someone wake me?"

"You're a guest," Mrs. Alexander answered. "Here you go."

"Looks wonderful. I could get used to this."

"Enjoy," Jessica Alexander encouraged, taking a seat across from Lisa at the table. "My boy's fond of you."

"I think highly of Steven," Lisa said cautiously. "You must be proud of him. He's a real asset to our company."

Jessica studied Lisa intently. This made Lisa uncomfortable.

"When will Marnie and Bill arrive?"

"They will join us for lunch. Marnie's anxious to see Steven. They have always been close," Jessica explained.

"I'm sure you're excited about your daughter's marriage," Lisa replied.

"We are pleased," Jessica said earnestly. "I'm glad you could come."

"I wouldn't have missed it. You have a lovely family."

"Thank you."

After breakfast, Lisa asked, "Can I help with the dishes?"

"They're done. Let's have coffee in the living room."

"Great." Lisa followed.

"Tell me about yourself?" Jessica encouraged.

"I graduated from UCLA and moved to Texas in July. My father recently --"

"I'm sorry to hear about your father," Jessica interjected, shaking her head. "How do you feel about Steve?"

"We've known each other only a short time," Lisa hedged. "Why do you ask?"

"Because my son is important to me. He's crazy about you," Jessica began. "Are you stringing him along?"

"Jessica, you are frank," Lisa replied, flabbergasted. "To answer your question, no. I'm fond of Steven."

"He thinks the sun does not set nor rise without your permission. I don't want to see him hurt."

"I wouldn't hurt Steven for the world. He's everything a woman could want."

"Good. I won't have you break his heart."

A knock at the door captured Jessica's attention. "Excuse me."

Lisa was relieved by the short reprieve. She felt as though she was being interrogated.

"Marnie and Bill are here," Jessica announced.

A dark-haired woman approached Lisa and embraced her as though she hadn't seen Lisa in years.

"Lisa, I'm Marnie. I'm so glad you could come. You've made Steven and me very happy."

"You're too kind."

"Hello, Lisa. I'm Bill Waters, Marnie fiancée. She's been anxious to meet you."

"Never mind Bill, he's prone to exaggeration," Marnie supplied. "Hello, momma."

"How are you sweetheart?" Jessica inquired.

"Fine. Where's Steven?

"He's helping your father. They'll be here for lunch."

"Momma, I stopped by the church," Marnie began."Everything's going to be beautiful."

At that moment, the front door opened. Mr. Alexander and Steven entered. Lisa could not believe the transformation clothes made. Steven looked like a cowboy.

Steven approached Lisa and kissed her thoroughly. Evidently, he wanted to stake his claim. Caught off guard, she was submissive.

Releasing Lisa, Steven turned his gaze to Marnie. "Sis, you grow prettier every day."

Marnie blushed. Steven moved in her direction.

"You don't mean a word of it, but I love it," Marnie replied, hugging Steven. "Where's Curtis and Tommy? And Bobby Sue?"

"The boys will be here," Steven supplied, shifting his gaze to his mother.

"Bobby Sue sends her love. The twins are sick with the flu and she can't make it," Jessica explained.

"Oh, momma! Couldn't she get a babysitter? It's my wedding for heaven sakes!"

"I know," Jessica said approaching Marnie's side. "It couldn't be helped."

The men left the room to clean up for lunch.

Marnie talked incessantly of the rehearsal, the wedding Saturday and the reception.

Lisa felt like a member of the family. Steven remained at her side, occasionally he would squeeze Lisa's hand.

~****~

Randall could not believe what Louise told him. Surely Lisa would not leave town with Steven. *What was wrong with her?* He knew each time he held her in his arms how breathless she became. Then why was Lisa playing both sides of the fence?

The house was quiet tonight. Daniel and Louise were attending a play. Suddenly the large house was lonely and Randall was restless. *You're jealous of Steven! Ridiculous!* What is it about Lisa that attracts you? You cannot predict her. She's her own woman – soft and beautiful. He wanted to protect her. His thoughts reverted to Steven. *I'm going to punch him out!*

~****~

"Lunch looks good, Mom," Walter Alexander stated, lifting a fork to his mouth.

"Thank you, dear," Jessica acknowledged.

"What time's the rehearsal?" Steven asked.

"Four o'clock," Curtis answered.

"How are you both getting along?" Marnie questioned, her gaze centered on Steven and Lisa.

Steven squeezed Lisa's hand and moved an arm around her. "We're just fine," he said, smiling.

"When will you tie the knot?" Marnie prodded. "We could make it a double ceremony."

Lisa blushed and stared down at her plate.

"Marnie, don't embarrass the gal," Walter scolded. "This is her first time here."

"Okay, daddy," Marnie conceded.

"I remember when we used to picnic by the lake," Curtis interjected.

"I always enjoyed them," Marnie agreed.

"Bill, you're a lucky man. You are marrying into a good family," Curtis said, attempting to change the subject.

"I couldn't agree more," Bill said, kissing Marnie's hand.

That afternoon, the rehearsal went well. The church was filled to capacity with floral arrangements.

Marnie was breath-taking in her old-fashioned gown and long train. Her dark hair and creamy complexion glowed, almost bringing tears to Lisa's eyes. Glancing around the room, Lisa noticed Jessica's eyes held unshed tears. Steven stood proudly as he watched Marnie walk down the aisle. The Alexanders exuded love -- Lisa could feel
it. Each member's joys and heartaches were shared by the entire family. Even elderly Aunt Clara, cranky as she was, was catered to
by everyone.

"As promiscuous as people are nowadays, I'm surprised anyone goes through with the ceremony at all," Aunt Clara grumbled.

"They love one another," Steven replied.

"Eh?" Aunt Clara said, leaning toward Steven.

"I said they weren't promiscuous. They love one another," Steven said loudly. Aunt Clara's deafness made him speak louder than usual.

The entire group turned to look at Steven and his elderly aunt in silence.

Moments later, everyone burst into laughter.

"Damn it anyway," Steven muttered.

"You mustn't use profanity," Clara scolded.

Steven took a deep breath and sighed. His lips thinned and his jaw set firmly.

"You ought to be ashamed," Clara babbled. "A tall good-looking man your age, should take on the responsibilities of a wife and family."

"Aunt Clara, please," Steven managed. Lisa chuckled. Steven gazed in Lisa's direction from the corner of his eyes. Shifting her gaze to scan the room, Lisa tried to look reserved.

Saturday arrived and Marnie's wedding was everything it had promised to be. Walter gave her away. Jessica and Lisa cried, as most of the women – even Aunt Clara. The reception was held at the Alexander home.

Lisa wasn't sure how it happened but she caught the bridal bouquet. Everyone teased her about being the next to marry.

"You could do worse than my good-looking brother," Marnie said as she embraced Lisa. She was surprised how much Marnie liked her.

"Congratulations! You're a beautiful bride," Lisa cried. "I'm sure you'll be very happy."

Curtis and Tommy led Marnie away fighting over who would get the first dance. Lisa enjoyed the friendly banter.

Steven touched Lisa's elbow and ushered her onto the dance floor as a slow tune began.

"You're family is enchanting. Look! Your parents are dancing," Lisa exclaimed.

"I thought everyone enjoyed their family as much as we have," Steven said.

"No. You're fortunate. Your family loves you very much."

"I'm a lucky man." Steven gathered her closer. "I love you, Lisa."

"I'm sure with the excitement and bubbly, you think so."

"Aunt Clara was right."

"What?" Lisa cast Steven a puzzled look.

"She says it's time a man my age acquires the responsibility of a wife and family," Steven explained with a grin. His mouth covered hers possessively. Everyone clapped.

The sudden applause caused Lisa to lift her head."I hope you're satisfied. We've made a spectacle of ourselves!"

Sheepishly, he grinned as he drew her into his arms. Whispering into her ear, "Lisa, will you marry me?"

Her brown eyes grew wide. Abruptly, Lisa's heart caught in her throat.

"What's wrong?" Steven asked with concern. "You look pale."

Presently, Curtis whirled Lisa around. "May I have this dance?"

She nodded in amazement.

"Lisa --" Steven said anxiously.

"Be a good sport," Curtis chided. "It's only a dance."

Saved by the bell! Lisa thought.

"What were the two of you so serious about?" Curtis inquired.

"Oh, nothing," Lisa hedged. "Marnie looks great."

"Yeah, sure," Curtis said in disbelief.

~****~

CHAPTER 9

The reception lasted well into the night. Lisa danced with most of the male guests and her feet ached. She deliberately avoided Steven, biding time in an attempt to stall. She wanted to handle this in a delicate manner.

Lisa feigned a headache. After bidding everyone goodnight, she retired for the night. Steven looked both concerned and hurt that she had not addressed his proposal, Lisa reflected in bed that night.

~****~

"Randall! Son, come in here for a moment," Daniel called from the hallway as he entered the house.

Randall stepped through the door of the study. "That you, Dad?"

"I thought for awhile you'd gone to bed," Daniel commented.

Randall was dressed for bed. "No. I had some contracts to go over for in the morning," Randall sighed. "Did you have a good time?"

"Better than that!" Daniel exclaimed. "Sit down, son. I've some wonderful news."

"I know, you've redone your will?" Randall asked.

"Oh that, bah!"

"Then what?"

"C'mon, sit down."

"Okay, I'm sitting. What's the big mystery?"

"You and I both know that since your mother died, this house has missed a woman's touch," Daniel began.

"Yes," Randall said, cautiously. This statement was out of character for his father. He listened intently. "What's this leading to?" he queried.

"Wouldn't you like to have a woman in the house again? A mother?" Daniel asked reluctantly.

"I'm a grown man. What are you talking about?"

"I've asked Louise to marry me. What's more, she has agreed," Daniel boasted. "I feel like a young man."

"What?" Randall could not believe what he was hearing. "Are you sure about this?"

"As sure as my name is Daniel Barryman."

"When did this happen?"

"Tonight. I thought we'd throw a party to announce our engagement."

"I'd like a drink," Randall began. "What'll you have?"

"A scotch on the rocks."

"Coming up." Randall crossed the room to the bar. "I don't believe this!"

"I should have realized this sooner," Daniel replied.

"In any event, here's to you and Louise," Randall offered a toast.

Daniel moved his glass to meet Randall's.

Randall was dumfounded. He knew he should be happy for his father, but the news caught him off guard, he couldn't think rationally.

"I'll have Mrs. Peterson make the invitations for next Saturday. Let's see, we'll invite Lena and Clarissa Roberts, Judge Parsons and his wife, the Alberts, Carlsons, and so on."

His father's words grew faint as Randall's mind began to wander.

"What do you think?," Daniel repeated.

"About what?"

"Do you think we should hire a band?"

"Of course, we'll hire the best," Randall replied. "There's been excitement enough for one day. You'd better get some rest."

"You're right. Good night son."

"Night, dad. Congratulations."

~****~

"Welcome back, Miss Franklin," Kim greeted. "How was the wedding?"

"It was beautiful," Lisa responded. "But it's good to be in Houston."

"Your messages are on the desk."

Lisa learned the office was quiet while she was away. Nevertheless she still had the problem of what to do about Steven's proposal. He had not pressed the issue.

"Telephone, Miss Franklin," Kim announced on the intercom. "It's your aunt."

"Hello, Louise," Lisa greeted. "I'm sorry, I missed you last night."

"That's fine dear. How are you?" Louise's voice was that of a teenager.

"I'm fine. What's up?" Lisa knew her aunt had something on her mind. Ordinarily Louise never called the office.

"I've the best news. You'll never guess."

"Okay. I give."

"I'm getting married," Louise's voice almost sang over the wire.

"Stop kidding around Louise."

"It's no joke. I'm serious."

"For heavens sakes, who?"

"Daniel Barryman."

There was a pregnant silence. Lisa felt as if someone had thrown a bucket of ice water in her face.

"The least you could do is, be happy for me," Louise said impatiently.

Jerking herself back to the present, Lisa said, "I'm sorry. Of course, I'm happy for you. I was stunned by the news. Congratulations."

"That's more like it. I want you to be my matron of honor."

"I'd love to."

"Daniel called and he's planned the engagement party for next Saturday. You'll be there?"

"Absolutely." Lisa made an effort to sound light-hearted. She knew this would mean seeing Randall again. She wasn't sure her heart could withstand the challenge.

"I just wanted you to know," Louise continued. "I've a million things to do, I'll see you tonight. Bye dear."

Just as Lisa hung up, the intercom buzzed.

"Miss Franklin, Mr. Ferguson is on line two. He says it's important," Kim informed.

"Hello, Mr. Ferguson," Lisa greeted with a smile in her voice. "How may I help you?"

"I think, someone should," Mr. Ferguson growled.

"I beg your pardon?"

"I've tried to reach you several times, young lady," Mr. Ferguson said impatiently.

"I'm sorry, I missed you," Lisa placated. "What can I do for you?"

"The ideas your office sent over are absurd."

"I don't understand," Lisa said in a controlled voice.

"I suggest a meeting. Let's discuss the problems."

"I certainly hope so," Mr. Ferguson said, agitation edging his voice. "I'm paying good money --"

"Calm down, Mr. Ferguson." Lisa said in a soothing tone. "Let me review your file and we'll get to the bottom of this."

"The earliest I can meet with you is, Thursday at ten o'clock."

What happened the short time she had been away? She had walked into turmoil. Louise would marry Daniel Barryman of all people! What set Mr. Ferguson off? Someone should outlaw Mondays. Coffee! Perhaps another cup would set her brain in motion. There was also the problem with Steven. What was she to do? He called in sick today. Maybe he regretted the proposal as much as she. Lisa poured a cup of coffee, then settled back into a chair. The correspondence on her desk begged for attention. A pile of bills had to be paid. Sipping her coffee, Lisa tackled the tasks one at a time.

Louise's engagement party was planned for this Saturday – good grief! She would have to face Randall. In fact, she would have to see him on a regular basis. Fate seemed determined to bring them together. Lisa never wanted to see Randall again.

~****~

"That does it, sir," Mrs. Peterson said.

"You'll drop them off in the mail at lunch?" Daniel questioned.

"Yes, sir. Everyone should have the invitations by tomorrow or the next day."

"It's rather short notice," Daniel uttered more to himself.
"Sir, I suggest we telephone the guests who live out of the area," Mrs. Peterson supplied.

"You're quite right." Daniel's mood improved. "Mrs. Martin will telephone the out-of- town guests."

The following day, Lena Roberts opened the mail and found the wedding invitation. "I don't believe it!" She proceeded to telephone Clarissa.

Clarissa was aghast with the news. "Louise Martin is marrying Daniel Barryman?" she repeated.

"That's what I said," Lena replied. "Who would have thought the old bird capable. His health is poor."

Clarissa would have to act fast if she wanted to prevent Lisa from worming her way into Randall's family.

~****~

The Barryman home buzzed for the entire week with preparations. The telephone rang frequently. The news stirred the local gossips, Randall considered. Daniel was giddy as a teenager. He knew Lisa would be at the wedding on Saturday. If he did not make an appearance at the engagement party, his father would never forgive him. But he did not want to see Lisa! Maybe she felt the same and would not attend. After what happened in California, Randall had had his fill of mouthy females. There were easier prey.

~****~

Wednesday morning, Lisa found a message on her desk that read:

Lisa, I am unable to keep our appointment Thursday. I have been called out of town. Regards, Mr. Ferguson.

One less problem to deal with this week, Lisa thought.
Although she could not imagine why he would be unhappy. Everything appeared to be in order, in fact the package they
offered him was attractive.

Saturday evening, Louise changed clothes several times and fretted with her hair, Lisa felt like screaming. Her aunt was not the only one ill at ease. Lisa had trouble describing the way she felt. She
wanted to be a million miles away.

Finally Louise settled on what she would wear and the women departed. As Malcolm drove closer to the Barryman home, Lisa felt as though she crashed head first into a brick wall. This was worse than she anticipated. Louise chattered like a young hen on the way over. Lisa managed to tune her out.

"We're here. C'mon dear," Louise repeated. "If I didn't know better I would think you're the one getting married."
Lisa stepped from the car and followed Louise.

"Good evening Mrs. Martin. Lisa."

"It's good to see you," Lisa said pleasantly.

"Hello Mrs. Peterson," Louise greeted. "Where's everyone?"

"Follow me please."

A long buffet table was set attractively Lisa thought. Soft track lights set the mood and everyone was dressed semi-formally. A
crowd of seventy-five to one hundred were present, she thought.
A jazz group played, *Thanks for the Memories*. Gazing nervously about, Lisa tried to relax. She failed to see Randall anywhere. The large Mediterranean home was alight with a spiral staircase and expensive paintings adorned the white stucco walls. Mrs. Peterson led the women to where Daniel was.

"Hello sweetheart," Daniel greeted as he moved to embrace Louise. "Welcome, Lisa. We're pleased you could make it." Daniel moved an arm possessively around Louise.

"Congratulations, Mr. Barryman," Lisa said with a broad smile.

"Call me Daniel. When you get to be my age --"

"Daniel it is," Lisa interjected.

"Have a drink?" Daniel offered.

"I'll have a glass of dry sherry, darling," Louise responded.

"A strawberry daiquiri for me," Lisa added.

Daniel walked over to the bar. Moments later he returned with their drinks.

With trepidation, Lisa downed her drink and crossed over to the bar. The bartender looks like a weight lifter Lisa considered. Male appreciation gleamed in his eyes.

"What'll you have?" the bartender asked.

"Another strawberry daiquiri, please."

"Are you here alone?"

"No," Lisa answered flatly. Accepting her drink, she turned and walked away. She almost collided with Steven talking to Clarissa.

"Well, look who's here," Clarissa purred.

"Hello, Lisa," Steven said with a forced smile.

"Hello Clarissa and Steven. How are you?" Lisa inquired smoothly, taking a sip of her drink.

"Steven was telling me about Austin," Clarissa volunteered.

"Yes. The wedding was very nice," Lisa said with aplomb.

"May I have this dance?" Steven asked.

Heaving a sigh, Lisa managed, "I thought you'd never ask! You'll excuse us, Clarissa?"

"Would you like to dance?" a tall blonde young man, who approached Clarissa asked.

"Absolutely," Clarissa said with a throaty laugh.

Subconsciously, Lisa scanned the crowd for Randall.

Drawing her close, Steven said, "I'm glad you made it. You look beautiful. You're wearing your hair different. I like it up." His words were incongruent with the signals his eyes sent.

"Thank you," Lisa murmured. "I thought it time for a change."

"You've avoided me since Austin," Steven accused.

Lisa opened her mouth to speak, then clamped shut.

"Don't deny it. I've racked my brain to figure what I had done," Steven added. "And you know what?"

Reluctantly, Lisa listened.

"I've done nothing," he said, his voice increased in volume. "At first it hurt because I care a great deal for you, then it hit me."

"What was your revelation?" Lisa inquired smoothly.

"You're in love with Barryman," Steven said icily. His look might have bored a hole through Lisa. A sick grin worked on his face.

"You've had to much to drink," Lisa accused.

"No," Steven denied. "You know that Randall is no good. He uses women like kleenex. He couldn't hope to appreciate a woman of your caliber. And just maybe I won't be around to pick up the pieces!"

"That's about enough!" Lisa said waspishly. She tried to break free of his grasp, but Steven tightened his grip. He's intoxicated or he wouldn't speak in this manner, she considered.

Steven had figured it out. It was a small wonder he had not pressed the subject further. Daniel and Louise were dancing closely. At least someone was happy, Lisa thought.

Where was Randall? Lisa wondered.

The slow tune ended. Lisa sighed as she closed her eyes briefly, then opened them. Across the room, her gaze riveted on Randall. He walked casually downstairs as the band began to play, *Bewitched, Bothered and Bewildered*. As though he possessed radar, Randall's eyes fixed on Lisa. He approached Steven and tapped his shoulder.

At first Steven appeared agitated, but stepped aside. Randall drew Lisa into his arms. He twirled Lisa to the music, and she was convinced her stomach was in the background somewhere. His hand was firm at her low back, his eyes inscrutable. Randall never uttered a word. Lisa felt at home in his arms. He's gorgeous – *Lord help me*! Randall was an accomplished dancer. Lisa could easily follow his lead. She loved this man.

He whisked Lisa onto the patio. His lips brushed her neck, tempting, and tantalizing her. He's too confident. *Damn him*, she thought.

"You're like a breath of fresh air," Randall said huskily.

"I thought you were out of town," she managed without sounding too breathless.

"Why did you leave California without a word?" he questioned softly.

"I thought it best under the circumstances," Lisa responded cautiously.

"You bewitch me and refuse to give me solace?"

"I wish I could believe that."

"You doubt me? Why?"

"Women come too easily for you. No wonder you never take any of it seriously," she explained.

"I take you seriously," Randall added with a provocative grin.

Lisa sighed in exasperation. "Men like you aren't meant to settle for one woman. You'd never be happy."

"Give me a chance. I'll grow on you after awhile," Randall murmured softly.

"You're to smooth for me." Momentarily Lisa thought she saw frustration flicker in his eyes, then just as quickly, a smirk replaced it.

"What do you think about Louise and Dad marrying" Randall queried.

"I hope they'll be happy."

The song, *It Never Entered My Mind*, began. Randall ushered Lisa into the garden. Possessively, his lips claimed hers.

Raining kisses over her neck and shoulder he said, "You're mine. I'll never let you go." His hands moved her hips flush with his. "Admit it Lisa," Randall challenged. "You missed me."

No response followed.

Randall's ragged breaths matched hers. "Lisa, I need you."

Caught in the heady experience, Lisa spiraled into space. Her feet were no longer susceptible to gravity.
Steven was intoxicated and angry, so he decided to fight fire with fire. Clasping Clarissa's hand, Steven led her onto the dance floor.

"Steven," Clarissa gasped. "I never knew you had it in you."
Consumed by curiosity, Clarissa suggested they get some fresh air. Just as they arrived on the patio, they saw Randall and Lisa locked in an embrace.

Steven fumed. He wanted to punch Randall's lights out. Instead, he growled, "C'mon, it's a crowded out here!" Steven lead Clarissa inside. She noticed Steven's face turned crimson on the patio.

With the unexpected intrusion, Randall and Lisa turned.

"Steven --!" Lisa managed.

Steven made a half turn, and glared at her, then continued inside with Clarissa in hand. He had had enough! Clarissa was available and he was tired of chasing Lisa. If she wanted the creep, she was welcome to him. He feared she would have to learn the hard way. And just maybe, he wouldn't be around to pick up the pieces!

Steven ushered Clarissa through the crowd. They stopped briefly to excuse themselves from the party. Everyone stared after them in amazement.

"Where are you taking me?" Clarissa bellowed. "You're hurting my arm!"

"We're going for a drive," Steven explained.

"Where?"

"Your place," Steven answered flatly.

"What's this all about ?" Clarissa asked, her temper flaring.

"This." Steven planted his mouth firmly over hers.

"Oh, Steven." Clarissa melted. "I had no idea." She smiled as he started the Acura's engine.

"It's time we became acquainted," he remarked huskily. Steven knew the liquor released his usual restraint, but he did not care. He was hurting and needed female companionship. He had been a patient man, but he had not been with a woman in six months.

When they discovered Lisa and Randall on the patio, Clarissa thought Steven reacted strangely. Later she discovered he really could kiss! Clarissa liked the new Steven. She always thought he was too good to be true. She knew both of them reacted to the scenario on the patio, but Clarissa could care less.

Lisa was aghast when she saw the contempt in Steven's eyes. "Oh, no," Lisa said more to herself.

"It's time Steven faced the facts," Randall remarked with a Cheshire grin.

"That's easy for you to say."

"Let the poor devil off the hook," Randall said, smiling. "He knows how you really feel about him."

Randall was right. Lisa had not meant to hurt him. She was totally confused. Poor Steven! she thought.

~****~

**CHAPTER 10**

"He'll never speak to me again," Lisa cried.

"Oh come on Lisa. I can't bear to see you cry," Randall muttered as he rocked her in his arms.

"He's been so nice and patient with me and I've," she wailed.

Randall wanted to protect her. Was he in love with her? Ridiculous! Damn! He hated to see Lisa cry.

"What's wrong son?" Daniel questioned as Randall approached with Lisa in hand.

"I'll handle it, Dad. Don't let this ruin your party. She'll be fine, I promise."

Directing her toward the door, Randall escorted her to his car.

Well she had done it again, made a scene! Lisa knew she would never live down the embarrassment. Everyone knew. She was glad to leave.

"Thank you, Randall," she sniffled "I appreciate you taking me home."

"Here, dry your face." Randall gave her his handkerchief.

"This isn't the way to Louise's home," Lisa remarked as he directed the car onto the freeway. "Where are we going?"

"Galveston."

"You need to get away. And I want some time alone with you," Randall explained as his foot depressed the accelerator.

"Why Galveston?"

"I bought a house in Pirate's Cove. We'll stay there for the weekend."

An hour later, the Ferrari pulled into the driveway of a three-storied beach house on Galveston Bay.

"C'mon, Lisa," Randall said as he offered his hand. She stepped from the car.

After opening the front door, Randall turned on the lights. "Well, what do you think?"

"It's beautiful," Lisa said glancing around the house. "What compelled you to buy it?"

"When I found out Dad was remarrying. Make yourself comfortable. I'll make us a drink."

Lisa kicked off her shoes and arranged herself on the sofa. Not bad, she thought. The man definitely has taste. The beach house was Art Deco in design.

Randall opened the French doors. The breeze blowing through felt good to Lisa. This was one of the advantages of living on the water.

"Here this will help," Randall coaxed, offering Lisa a drink.

"What is it?"

"Dry sherry."

One could relax here, she thought. She would follow her instincts from now on. No more being afraid to take a chance.

"What are you thinking?" Randall asked, his voice was like a soft caress.

"How happy I am to be here with you," she confessed.

A remote control laid on the coffee table. Randall picked it up and pushed a button. Tchaikovsky's, *Swan Lake*, played on the stereo.

"I'm pleased," he said moving closer.

"Thanks for rescuing me tonight," Lisa said more for lack of knowing what to say. He made her nervous when he looked at her that way.

"Anytime." Randall's mouth covered hers. Leaning closer, he pushed her back against the pillows and placed one knee between hers, as a result her dress moved up her thighs.

"You're beautiful," he whispered as he rained kisses over her neck and shoulders. "I can't seem to keep my hands off you."

Her defenses lowered, Lisa unbuttoned his shirt and moved her hands along his rib cage. Shifting her position, she allowed Randall to remove her dress and brassiere.

"Oh Lisa," Randall murmured. "I've wanted you so."

"Take me."

Her words pleased Randall, his hand arched over a soft mound. Trailing his tongue upward from her navel to her breasts, Randall spread liquid fire through Lisa.

"Oh, Randall." A soft moan escaped her as Randall took her nipple in his mouth. His tongue circled, teasing.

"Do you like that, babe?"

"Oh yes!" she sighed. His touch heightened her sensibilities. Her pulse bounded with excitement. From the center of her being, her body cried for relief.

He ached for Lisa. Randall had waited too long. He knew if he did not possess her soon, he would be in great pain.

Lisa felt his swelling desire as he shifted his weight.

Randall tossed two cushions onto the floor and rose. He struggled out of his pants and motioned for her to join him on the floor. He could not wait any longer. He took her.

Lisa snuggled into his embrace. She felt the fireworks explode within her. Randall's possession catapulted them skyward, tumbling and dipping them, as one.

He could not get his fill of her. Randall was convinced he never would. Again he sent them spiraling into the heavens.

As the tides grew calm, Randall took a deep breath before rolling onto his back. He was content with this woman at his side. Lisa was his woman. Lisa moved to his side, resting her head on his shoulder.

"You'll have to give me a few minutes," he whispered. "I'm not what I used to be." He laughed.

Lisa shook her head. "I just want to be near you."

"Happy?" He kissed her forehead.

"Immensely."

He grasped her hand and moved it to his mouth, as he placed a kiss. "I'm starved," he whispered. "For food."

"What's in the fridge?" she asked. "I could throw something together ."

"Unfortunately, I hadn't planned to be here," he confessed. "We'll have to go out. Do you mind?"

Lisa doubted anything would ever bother her again. Shaking her head, she responded, "C'mon, I'll race you to the shower!"

Randall threw his head back and laughed heartily. She stood up, and for a few moments Lisa gazed down at him. He was the perfect male. She loved him. Lisa would accept whatever he offered her. Being with Randall, she admitted was her heart's desire.

She has a strange expression, he thought. Her soft curves and planes, dark hair cascading down her back and full breasts, reminded him of Lady

Godiva. She threw a pillow at him and ran out of the room, giggling. His content expression quickly changed to surprise when the pillow landed in his face.

"Okay, so you want to play!" He pushed to his feet. After a few trips around the sofa, he cornered her, then lunged forward.

She broke free of his grasp and sent them sprawling across the sofa, then onto the floor in laughter.

His eyes became darkened pools, his body tensed. Randall raised on elbows and leaned forward brushing his lips tenderly against hers. Exhaling deeply, he withdrew. "We'd better go or I'll never eat again." He stood and offered his hand, she accepted it. They took a shower, dressed and left shortly.

Randall drove to the market since Lisa insisted on cooking for them. He was having the time of his life. Randall imagined how life would be with her every day. Don't get too domestic, he scolded himself.

Settling over a chef's salad, Randall commented, "Tell me about your family."

"There's not much to tell," Lisa remarked casually.

"You mentioned you didn't know your father very well."

"He divorced my mother for another woman. Mother never quite recovered."

"There were hard feelings?"

"That's putting it mildly."

"Did you like West Texas and ranch life?

"Of course. My grandparents raise cattle, horses and ostrich."

"Ostrich?"

"Yes, they're raised for leather, their feathers are used for decorating. A few ranchers have started to raise ostrich, others raise zebras, gnu and gazelles because there's money to be made on exotic animal products. West Texas climate is similar to the Serengeti Plains of northern Tanzania."

"I see. Sounds like you enjoyed it."

"My grandparents are wonderful people, " Lisa mused.

"You never mention your mother."

"She died in an auto accident when I was fifteen."

"What was she like?"

"An unhappy woman."

"I'm sorry. I didn't mean to pry."

"It used to bother me, but she lived her life the way she wanted," Lisa commented."How about your family?"

"My mother was the typical, beautiful socialite. She enjoyed parties, travel and my father," he remarked. "My father lived to please her."

"What do you remember most about your childhood," Lisa managed.

"School."

"School?" Lisa repeated in amazement.

"Yes, I attended the best boarding schools. My father used to say a person without training in proper etiquette, culture and education made him shudder," Randall said with more than a tinge of anger in his voice. His brows furrowed with the recollection.

"You went home for the holidays, I imagine," Lisa offered cheerfully.

"Sure. When they had nothing else planned." A shadow crossed his face. Suddenly, he seemed distant and unapproachable. Moments later, he forced his best smile. "We'd better rest. It has been a full day."

Sunday they made love until noon. Afterward, Randall insisted they go for a swim. Later, that night Lisa prepared dinner for them.

He accompanied her into the kitchen and observed her with the silliest grin she thought.

On the return trip to Houston, Randall was dark and brooding. She tried to tease him out of his dark mood, however he remained silent as if he carried the weight of the world on his shoulders.

Finally she could stand it no longer, Lisa asked, "Is there something wrong? You've scarcely said a word."

"What will you tell Steven?"

His question caught Lisa off guard. "Steven? About what?"

"He's in love with you. Any fool can see that!"

"Yes. He asked me to marry him."

"Have you slept with him?"

Lisa didn't care for the tone of his voice. He sounded as though he was entitled to know.

"That's none of your business!"

Randall shot her a look of disapproval, once again the autocratic Randall Barryman. *Who does he think he is?* She never asked him intimate questions.

He took the next exit off the freeway and slammed on the brakes. The movement sent Lisa forward, then back again in the seat.

"What's wrong with you?" she hissed.

"I want an answer and I want it, now!" Randall demanded, his grasp tightening on her upper arms.

He can wait until hell freezes over! she thought. He's a chauvinistic autocrat.

"I told you, that's none of your business," Lisa repeated firmly. "Now, take your hands off me!"

She knew sparks would fly. Once again they would be at one another's throats. Lisa hoped she was wrong. The relationship would never work. He has the temperament of a Tasmanian devil! Some things would never change.

Randall stared a hole through her for an extended moment, then he released her. He moved to the driver's side and lit a cigarette. Lisa was too astonished. She failed to see the trembling of his hands.

After a few puffs, he pressed the cigarette out in the ashtray. Impassively he said, "I'll take you home."

She wanted to cry but refused to let him know how he affected her. Ignoring him, Lisa pressed her face to the passenger window. The rest of the trip was in pregnant silence.

At long last, the automobile stopped in front of the Martin home. Lisa grabbed the door handle and pushed, then swung her legs out. Slamming the door, she walked toward the house.

"Lisa-- !"

She never turned nor broke her stride. She could hear tires squeal as they contacted the pavement as Randall pulled from the driveway.

~****~

Monday morning, Lisa dreaded seeing Steven and the unfinished business with Mr. Ferguson. Circumstances were difficult before and she always persevered. She would again!

Lisa found a note on her desk informing her Mr. Ferguson wanted to meet with her today. Terrific! she thought. Why did problems, usually the worst kind, happen on Monday? She poured a cup of coffee, then worked to psyche herself up for the meeting at ten.

Then she remembered, Steven. Surely he would attend the meeting.

Steven entered the doorway, a folder in hand. He had the semblance of a smile on his face. "We need to talk before Mr. Ferguson arrives," he said politely.

"Please come in," Lisa encouraged.

"I've reviewed the Ferguson account with his office. It appears they did not receive the final package we sent. Instead, a switch was made."

"How did this happen?"

"I learned Clarissa has a friend who works for Mr. Ferguson. She substituted some cockamamie ideas to make us look bad," Steven explained.

"Why would she do such a rotten thing?"

~****~

**CHAPTER 11**

"First of all, she doesn't want to share the spotlight. Second, she thinks you're out to steal Randall from her, so she has set out to ruin you – personally and professionally. She has spread lies about us. You, in particular."

"I'll strangle her!" Lisa said emphatically.

"Forget her for now. Here's what we'll do."

Promptly at ten o'clock, a gruff Mr. Ferguson entered Lisa's office.

"Please have a seat, Mr. Ferguson," Steven said casually.

"It's good to see you," Lisa added, a broad smile covered her face.

"I wish I could say the same. I'm aghast at the presentation you've offered. A child could have done better!"

"Sir, I can clear up the whole matter," Steven began. "There's been a mistake."

"I don't follow," Mr. Ferguson interjected.

"A new member of our staff sent out the wrong portfolio," Steven answered smoothly. "We would like to apologize for the inconvenience and confusion. Sketchy ideas for another project were submitted in error."

"In that case --" Mr. Ferguson was at loss for words.

"We assume full responsibility for the delay and we'll adjust our fees accordingly," Steven finished. "We hope you won't think badly of us, sir? We value your account."

"Not at all," Mr. Ferguson commented, rising. "You'll see to the details, Steven?"

"You can count on it," Steven responded. The men shook hands.

Lisa was impressed with Steven's finesse. He had turned an irate man into honey. She rose. "Thanks for coming by."

"Goodbye." Mr. Ferguson smiled and turned to depart.

As the door closed behind their client, Steven sat down and propped his feet on the desk. Clearly, he was pleased with himself.

"You saved the account. Thank you," Lisa said approvingly.

He smiled impishly.

"What is it?" she blurted out, inspecting the room for little green elves or men from outer space.

Silence.

"About Saturday night," Lisa began cautiously.

"Oh that! I've forgotten about Saturday," Steven dismissed.

"I thought you'd be furious. What gives?" Lisa's interest piqued.

"I'll admit, I was jealous and hurt at first," Steven confessed. "But I know you care for the guy. I'd still like to be your friend."

"I'm relieved." Lisa released a deep sigh. "Things are working out better than I had hoped. I don't want anything to destroy our friendship."

"Never," Steven responded. "You going to marry the lucky son-of-a -- ?"

"Steven!"

"Sorry. I lost my head. When will Louise marry?"

"They will be married in two weeks. Aunt Louise acts like a school girl. She's truly in love. It's wonderful."

"Daniel's marrying a fine lady," Steven added thoughtfully, "I hope you don't mind if I leave early today? I have some personal business to attend."

"After what you've done for the firm, no problem," Lisa answered with a broad smile.

She knew he was being evasive, but he was entitled to his privacy.

On the way out the door Steven said, "Incidentally I want to wish you and Randall well." The door closed silently behind him.

Steven was a helluva guy! He would make some woman a wonderful husband, she reflected. He had been noble about the whole thing.

Her thoughts turned to Randall. If only Steven knew, she had lost on both counts. But she would think about that tomorrow!

Later that evening, Louise was reviewing her list of wedding invitations when Lisa entered the Martin home.

"Hello, Aunt Louise," Lisa beamed, kissing her aunt's cheek.

Louise glanced up from her work, puzzled. "Whatever it is, I'm totally innocent!" Louise said playfully. Suspiciously she watched Lisa, half expecting her niece to announce she suffered from Alzheimer's or a brain tumor.

"Nothing's wrong. I'm happy for you," Lisa announced. Louise gazed up mutely.

"I know things looked bad Saturday, but today everything's wonderful!"

She has taken leave of her senses, Louise thought.

"Both of you disappeared Saturday. Daniel says Randall came home Sunday, as irritable as a caged lion."

Silence.

"What happened? It's as though you're guarding some dark secret," Louise continued.

"Suffice to say, troubled waters have stilled. I am so relieved. Tell me about your wedding plans."

Dismayed, Louise was sure she had missed some of the conversation along the way. "We thought we would have the ceremony at Daniel's home - - private, you know. I will wear pastel yellow. What do you think?" Louise crossed the room and held her wedding dress in front of her.

"You'll be the belle of the ball!"

Tears filled Louise's eyes. "You know just what to say."

"I mean it." Both women embraced.

"Thank you Lisa. I would be lost without you."

"Randall has bought a beach house in Galveston," Lisa said without much foresight.

"How do you know?"

"I spent the weekend with him," Lisa confessed.

"What's happening with you?" Louise asked emphatically. "We're so worried about you."

"I'm in love with Randall."

"And he doesn't return your affection?"

"He has feelings for me in his own way. He's not capable of committing to one person," Lisa sobbed. "He has the worst temper. He's domineering, autocratic, chauvinistic and a bully. All he does is pick fights. It's hardly a basis for a relationship."

"Life has a way of working out when you least expect it," Louise reassured. "I'm tired dear, think I'll go to bed."

~****~

"Miss Franklin, Clarissa Roberts is here to see you," Kim announced.

"Show her in," Lisa said reluctantly. *What could the troublemaker want?*

Lisa rose from her desk as Clarissa entered. "Good morning, Clarissa. What brings you here?"

"Hello," Clarissa said flatly. "We need to talk."

Lisa noticed one of Clarissa's high heels tapped the floor repetitively.

"You little witch! How could you?" Clarissa bellowed as she walked around the desk. Grabbing Lisa's hair, Clarissa dug in for a better grip.

Lisa screamed and pushed Clarissa, sending her across the room. A lamp fell to the floor, breaking. "Are you out of your mind?"

"Why don't you go back to California? You little witch!" Clarissa advanced. "I'll pull every hair out of that thick skull of yours!"

"Over my dead body," Lisa retorted. She had had her fill of Clarissa. Someone should teach her a lesson.

"That can be arranged," Clarissa hissed. They rolled locked in a tight embrace. Clarissa's hair tumbled out of its neat chignon.

"I'm the one who should be furious," Lisa accused. "You've spread lies about me and tried to ruin me."

Each held a firm grasp of the other, rolling across the floor with clothes in disarray, and hair tousled.

"Leave Randall alone unless you want to be bald-headed!" Clarissa snarled. "He's mine. You came here that innocent act and have started trouble. Well, I've had enough. I'm warning you!"

Lisa thought to calm down and stand up to Clarissa. "Or you'll?"

Abruptly the door opened, Randall entered.

"What's this about?" Randall growled. "You're acting like children." He pulled Clarissa off Lisa.

"Clarissa started it," Lisa said, breathing rapidly.

"You both should be ashamed! Two grown women," Randall ground out.

"Get out, Clarissa! And don't come back!" Lisa yelled.

Straightening her clothes, Clarissa preened herself and walked out of the room.

Sobbing, Lisa threw herself into his arms. "Thank goodness you're here!" she cried.

"She's gone and she'll never bother you again, I promise."

"She's a vengeful woman," Lisa said in disbelief. "I had no idea what lengths she would go. Clarissa plans to marry you."

"That's ridiculous," he reassured. "She's always been misguided."

"I hate her!"

"She's to be pitied. Clarissa wouldn't have acted this way if she weren't desperate," Randall explained.

"It must be horrible to care for someone who doesn't love you," Lisa exclaimed. "Have you ever been in love?"

"No," Randall replied.

His words hurt more than if she suffered a guillotine. "I'm sorry you had to witness that scene."

"It must have been awful for you," Randall offered.

"You have no idea."

"C'mon, I'll take care of you," Randall ordered.

"But --"

"You're coming with me," he announced.

At that moment, Kim entered Lisa's office poised to speak.

"Take a message, Kim," Randall instructed the secretary. Smiling, Kim nodded her acknowledgement.

"Ah --" Lisa began.

"Forget it," Randall ordered. "You're going home." He crossed over to liquor cabinet. "I know its early, but drink this."

"What?"

"Drink it!" he insisted.

Lifting the glass, she gulped its contents. It burned going down. It might have been strychnine for all she knew. He refilled the glass, and she emptied it.

She passed out. Randall carried her out of the office.

"Mr. Barryman, what happened?" Kim exclaimed. He inclined his head.

"It's okay, Kim." Randall placed Lisa over his shoulder and walked nonchalantly out of the office.

"Yes, sir."

That evening, Lisa woke. She raised on one elbow. She could not remember when she left the office or her whereabouts. This was not the Martin home. She arranged herself on the sofa. Okay, she told herself, back up some and remember. What happened? She felt strangely warm inside, relaxed.

Minutes later a familiar voice greeted her. "I see you've come around."

"Yes, where?" she stammered.

"You passed out in the office, so I brought you here," Randall supplied.

"Oh my, what will your father think?"

"He won't be home for hours, his meetings last forever. Afterward the men at the club are throwing him a bachelor party. How do you feel?"

"Warm, like maple syrup."

"Good. The sherry helped."

"Sherry?"

"Drastic circumstances require desperate measures."

"Why would you be carrying sherry with you?"

"To celebrate," he flashed a wolfish grin.

"What's the occasion?"

"I have a buyer for Las Palmas," he said proudly. "After the promotions Franklin Advertising has done, I received a call today. I thought you'd want to be the first to know," he muttered.

"That's wonderful. Congratulations."

"I was surprised to find you and Clarissa at one another's throats," he said moving closer.

"So was I."

"About Sunday, I never meant for us to part the way we did," Randall said softly, securing an errant tendril of black hair behind her ear.

"It's best forgotten."

"No, damn it!"

"You see? When we're together inevitably one of us loses their temper."

"I have an abominable temper -- always have," he admitted.

"That's no basis for a relationship. We both know it," Lisa said, rising. "Thanks for the rescue. I should go."

"No, please," he uttered. "Stay with me."

"I don't want an affair. We've had a good time and it's over. You have your life and I have mine."

"Just like that?" Randall prodded. "You have no feelings for me?"

"Of course I do."

His eyes pleaded with hers for understanding. "Lisa, I need to explore my feelings for you. Frankly, I 'm not sure how to deal with them."

"Life can be overwhelming at times. I'm confused as you are."

"Give us a chance. I've never depended on anyone. Now I have this strong urge and it scares the hell out of me."

"It's hormones," Lisa supplied.

"This isn't a laughing matter," he growled.

"I'm just trying to lighten your mood. You're so serious."

Deliberately, Lisa tried to sound cavalier about the whole incident. Inside, her heart was broken.

"You're right about one thing. I have a problem with commitment," Randall began reluctantly, his back to her, he stared at the family portraits on the mantel.

"Our relationship will never be more than an affair," Lisa said softly. "You mean well, but I don't think you're capable of commitment. It's your nemesis. I appreciate your honesty and I'll always treasure your friendship."

"Friendship? Never !" he said adamantly. "After what we've shared, I don't think so."

"Until the novelty wears off."

~****~

**CHAPTER 12**

Ignoring her words he said, "I've asked Mrs. Peterson to prepare dinner for us. Will you join me?" The dark clouds lifted from his face, Randall appeared himself once more.

"Yes, thank you."

Mrs. Peterson had outdone herself. The dinner table was covered with a crocheted tablecloth, and lit by candlelight. The red snapper, broccoli and scalloped potatoes were delectable. Lisa had a hard time taking her eyes off the man she loved. She thought she saw a wistful look in his eyes at times, as if he was contemplating an antidote for a feared virus.

After the meal, Randall crossed the room to the stereo and pushed a disc inside. A slow jazzy tune filled the room.

"Care to dance?"

Rising, Lisa moved into his arms. Randall hauled her to him, moving sensuously to the music. She fits next to me perfectly, he considered. He felt as though an earthquake occurred and he was hanging onto a tree limb for his life. If he let go, he would fall into the center of the earth. Randall did not release her as one tune ended and another began. He kissed her cheek and stroked her hair.

"Bewitched, bothered and bewildered am I," Randall sang the words along with the tune.

"You better watch it. Saying things you don't mean. Men have been shot for less."

"Do you know what it's like having you here?"

"Tell me."

"Heaven," he said, picking up the pace, whirling her to the music. Drawing Lisa closer, he kissed her thoroughly. Lisa was limp.

"My father and Louise will marry soon. Move in with me?" he suggested. "We need time together."

"You're asking me to be your mistress?"

"I wouldn't put it that way. Why is everything either black or white with you? Stop fighting me. Allow us some happiness."

"I want to, but I'm afraid."

"I won't hurt you. Nothing will as long as I'm around. He kissed her neck. "You're driving me crazy. I don't sleep nights for thinking of you," Randall whispered.

His statement filled Lisa with purpose.

"Well?"

She shot him a bewildered look.

"I want to take care of you."

"Like a pet?"

"C'mon Lisa, be serious. This is a big step for me. It's all I'm capable of right now."

Lisa gazed up mutely. Framing his face with both hands, she kissed him. He looked so vulnerable and sincere she considered.

"I'll think about it," she answered as she withdrew.

"Promise me one thing?" he whispered.

She nodded.

"You'll forgive my bad temper and allow me to see you?"

Lisa could forgive him anything, she reflected. *God, I love him!* "I will."

Taking her in his arms, Randall's head dipped. His tongue sparred with hers.

"Where would we live?" Lisa questioned. "Provided I agree."

"I've looked at some houses. I'll show them to you."

"Why do you have such a hang-up with commitment?" she asked. There, she said it. Every cell in her body went on alert for his answer.

"Do you know what it's like to stay awake nights, wondering why your parents didn't want you around?"

Lisa was dumfounded. "What?"

"I do."

~****~

"Did you get your personal business attended?" Lisa asked Steven in the office on Tuesday.

Steven responded with a knowing grin. "Yes."

"Why do I have a feeling you're keeping some dark secret from me?"

He laughed. "I suppose I should tell you."

"Please do. I'm dying of curiosity."

"When I learned Clarissa sabotaged the Ferguson account, I decided to call in a few favors. Let's just say, anyone can start gossip. Clarissa caught wind of it."

"No wonder she attacked me!"

"That cheap -- !" he barked.

"See what happens when you stoop to the same level. Where do you draw the line?"

"What happened with Clarissa?"

"Randall pulled her off me."

"She physically attacked you?"

"I was surprised as well."

"I'm sorry. However on a lighter note, out of this mess I met Julie, Mr. Ferguson's daughter. Boy, is she a number!"

"Men!" Lisa gave Steven a brotherly hug.

"So, tell me about her."

"She's tall, auburn hair and she's well, put together in all the right places," Steven laughed.

"Have you asked her out yet?"

"Yes, last night. It went rather well, too. I'm seeing her again tonight."

"That's great. I want you to be happy."

Lisa was relieved to find Steven had someone in his life, she reflected as she drove home after work.

"Good evening, Miss Lisa," the housekeeper greeted. "Miss Louise is in the parlor."

"Thank you, Mrs. Murphy." Lisa set her briefcase on the hall table.

"Lisa? Is that you?" Louise called from the other room.

"Yes, Aunt Louise. How's it going?"

"This completes the last of the preparations for the wedding," Louise said as she rose from her desk and stretched. "Did you have a good day?"

"You'll never guess, so I'll tell you. Steven has a girlfriend.

"Oh?"

"It's all quite hush, hush. Her name is Julie Ferguson. Isn't it wonderful?"

"Everyone has someone, except you Lisa."

"Don't start playing cupid. I'm not in the mood."

"You'd rather be an old maid?" Louise scolded mockingly.

"I'm twenty-eight hardly an old maid. We live in different times. Today women wait to marry until they're thirty."

"If I had children, you're the daughter I would have wanted," Louise said. Lisa embraced her aunt.

~****~

"Son, what are your intentions toward Lisa?" Daniel asked, a serious expression played on his face.

"Why do you ask?"

"I will not have you toy with her affections. She's different. A man could marry a woman like her. She has brains and beauty."

"Did Louise put you up to this?"

"She's too fine a lady to suggest anything this devious." Daniel winked.

Randall shook his head in disbelief.

"You haven't answered my question," Daniel repeated.

"That's between Lisa and me."

Forging ahead, Daniel inquired, "There's a problem?"

"Maybe."

"You're thirty-four, son. It's time to settle down and raise a family," Daniel prodded.

"Like you?" Randall said with a trace of bitterness in his voice. He glared at the older man.

"You've never forgiven your mother and me."

"It's hard to forget. Too many years have passed," Randall ground out.

"I'm not saying we were right. Just try to deal with the past, if not for me, for yourself."

"I used to get into to trouble just so you'd notice me." Randall scowled.

"We made many mistakes, son. I'll regret them until the day I die."

"You gave me everything but your time."

"We always loved you," Daniel defended.

"You had a damn funny way of showing it!"

"We were wrong, son. We were caught up in our own lives. I tried to give you all the advantages," Daniel said quietly.

"I just wanted your love. Not a trip to Europe," Randall's voice cracked.

"I know, son." Daniel moved toward Randall with open arms as Randall approached.

"I've always loved you. Damn proud of you too!" Daniel said, tears rolling down his cheeks.

"Dad, I love you too."

"We can't undo the past, but we can change the future," Daniel declared.

"So true."

"C'mon let's have a brandy," Daniel suggested.

~****~

Again Louise was right, Lisa reflected as she readied for bed. What was she waiting for? She loved a man not unlike her father -- a womanizer. Why couldn't she care for Steven? He had proposed and Lisa ran. Basically Lisa was happy, she did not want to become bitter and alone. What should she do about Randall? He wanted her as his mistress. He said he wasn't the marrying kind, and wanted no commitments. Could she settle for this and be happy? Lisa fantasized about the children they would have. The boy with brown, curly hair like Randall. *Don't torture yourself*, she chided.

The telephone rang.

"Hello?" Lisa answered.

"Oh, Lisa," a female voice cried.

"Who is this?"

"It's Marnie."

"What's wrong?"

"It's just awful."

"Calm down, Marnie."

"My marriage is over!" Marnie exclaimed. "I can't go home. My parents would never understand. Can I stay with you for awhile? Until I find a job?"

"I suppose so," Lisa replied. "Where are you?"

"Houston. I'll need directions."

An hour later, Lisa heard an automobile pull into the driveway as she glanced at the clock, it was nine o'clock. Lisa helped Marnie carry her bags inside.

"Your aunt won't mind if I stay?" Marnie questioned.

"Don't be silly." Lisa embraced her. "Care for some herbal tea?"

"Strawberry if you have it."

127

"My favorite too."

"What has happened?" Lisa inquired intently, sipping her tea.

"Daddy gave us twenty acres for a wedding present," Marnie began.

Lisa inclined her head.

"Everything was fine for awhile. Then Bill's old flame, who was recently widowed, moved nearby."

"So?"

"She's making a play for my husband," Marnie cried. He can't see past her large blue eyes. She controls him and he doesn't even know it. I refuse to live that way."

"You poor thing! Lisa sympathized. "Have you talked to your mother about this?"

"Momma would never understand."

"You're sure about this?"

"I wish I weren't!"

"My aunt will marry in a week. I'd planned to move anyway. We could room together," Lisa suggested.

"I can't thank you enough."

"Does Steven know you're here?"

"I want to find a job before I tell him."

"He'll be hurt if you don't tell him," Lisa warned.

Marnie scowled.

"It's your decision."

"Thanks." Marnie heaved a relieved sigh. "Where will I

sleep?"

"There's a guest room next to mine. C'mon."

She would help Marnie find a job tomorrow. Lisa's mind churned. Where would they live? It would be nice to have a roommate near her age. Perhaps in time, both would forget the men in their lives. Not everyone married and lived happily ever after, Lisa thought.

During breakfast, Lisa explained to Louise about Marnie. Her aunt accepted the news in stride. Lisa left for work at eight-thirty, still Marnie hadn't come down to breakfast. She had no idea what Marnie's skills were. She left a note for Marnie with Mrs. Murphy.

When Lisa arrived at the office, Kim had some letters for her signature, telephone messages to answer and problems to resolve with unhappy clients. By noon, Lisa's head was buzzing. Still, there was no word from Marnie.

A pile of unfinished work remained on Lisa's desk. She asked Kim to bring her a sandwich. At one o'clock, the telephone rang. Kim had not returned from lunch.

"Franklin advertising, may I help you?" Lisa greeted.

"Lisa! I suppose you thought I had disappeared?" Marnie greeted on the other end. "I was so tired I slept until noon. How's it going?"

"It has been a hectic day," Lisa said. "Rest today. I'll get a paper and we'll go over it tonight."

"Thanks, Lisa." Marnie rang off.

"Who was that?" Steven asked playfully, entering the room.

"Marnie," Lisa blurted without much forethought.

"Marnie?" Steven inquired. "Is she sick? Or the family?"

"No. Relax."

"What did she want?" Steven's voice was laced with concern.

"She's left Bill." Lisa felt like a snitch.

"Where is she?"

"Staying with us."

"Louise's house?"

"Until she finds a place of her own."

"I'm going to call her and find out what's happened.

"No! She asked me not to say anything until she finds a job."

~****~

**CHAPTER 13**

"This isn't like Marnie."

Lisa felt she had given it away, she might as well tell Steven the whole truth. "And that's not the whole story."

"Damn! I'll kill the son-a--!"

"You can't do that! What's Marnie trained to do?"

"She has an associate degree in computers. I'll ask around for her."

"How are things with Julie?" Lisa asked casually.

Steven smiled at the mention of her name. He looked pleased with himself. "Very well."

"Let Marnie handle her own problems, Steven."

"You're right of course."

Steven had to leave and he promised to let his sister contact him.

Briefly, Randall crossed Lisa's mind. She was immersed with Louise's wedding, Steven's new relationship and Marnie's unexpected arrival, she had no time to think of Randall. If only he wasn't a rake! Why hadn't he called? Lisa had no apparent answers. Why didn't he tell her he could not live without her? Demand she marry him? She knew situations like this only happened in romance novels.

When Lisa arrived at the Martin home, she was disappointed to find Randall had not telephoned. She discovered that Marnie and Louise had become fast friends. While Marnie and Louise chattered over the wedding plans, Lisa noticed Marnie would occasionally look pensive, shake her head and become teary.

After dinner Louise retired early that night. Lisa and Marnie decided to go for a swim. Floating on her back in the warm water, Lisa closed her eyes to relax.

"Do you have anyone special in your life," Marnie asked after surfacing the water.

"Yes. But it's a lost cause."

"Doesn't he care for you?" Marnie inquired. "You love him. I've seen the wounded look in your eyes."

Suddenly Lisa opened her eyes. "Is it that obvious?"

"Afraid so. Who is he?"

"His name is Randall. He's a rake, hardly husband material."

"You going to let him go? Is there another woman?"
"He denies it. He wants me to move in with him."

"Why didn't you tell me?"

"I have no plans to follow through. He has not telephoned. He probably regrets asking."

"How can you enjoy life if you're afraid to live it? There are no guarantees in life. Just go for the gusto!"

"You make it sound like a beer commercial," Lisa laughed. "So easy."

"It is. You have to grab the happiness life offers, when it's offered. The opportunity may never present itself again."

Lisa scoffed.

"Tell him you love him. Take a chance," Marnie coaxed. "Who wants to live in a bubble?"

"Good advice for both of us," Lisa smiled knowingly.

"I'll call Bill tomorrow," Marnie said.

~****~

Lisa was pleased when Marnie and Bill resolved their problems. She helped Lisa realize and deal with her fear of gambling on a relationship with Randall. Lisa always seemed to prefer a sure thing. A week passed and today was Louise's wedding. Over the past week, Lisa knew Randall would not call, and she refused to call him. Louise was beautiful in the lacy pastel yellow dress she wore, Lisa thought. She would see Randall at the wedding, there was no way to avoid it.

~****~

"You've been a bear all week! What's wrong?" Daniel asked, inspecting his reflection. "Rather dashing for a man of sixty-five."

"I have not," Randall said defensively. He knew he'd growled all week. Damn! Why wouldn't Lisa take him seriously? He had opened up to her. For what? She had not called him. And *like hell he would!* A man has his pride.

Daniel spared no expense with preparations. There were several large floral arrangements, the best catering service, bartenders, and an orchestra. Lisa would never forget the elaborate ceremony. Randall was Daniel's best man, and Steven gave Louise away. Randall's gaze fixed on Lisa as she walked down the aisle in the pastel yellow crepe de chine dress. His heart pounded in his chest and an overwhelming ache began in his midline. He was trembling – she's beautiful!

Struggle as she might Lisa remembered very little of the wedding, after seeing Randall. Lisa's gaze riveted on him. He keeps staring at me, she thought. His eyes were unreadable. Randall was probably relieved to be rid of her. Louise and Daniel kissed, then she threw the bouquet. To her amazement, Lisa caught it.

Randall smiled to himself as he approached Lisa. What would she say?

Why does he have that silly grin on his face? Lisa wondered. *Lord help me!*

"Hello, Lisa." Randall flashed a devastating smile.

She hesitated a moment, then said, "How are you? Lovely ceremony."

"Yes. Dance with me?" Randall interrupted.

"My pleasure."

She feels so good in my arms – she smells of jasmine. Randall pulled her closer than necessary.

Lisa was in trance-like state. He nuzzled her neck.

"Why haven't you called?" he asked softly.

No response followed.

"What's your answer? And don't pretend with me."

"My answer is no."

"Why?"

"I'll live with the man I marry," Lisa said gazing up at him.

"Looks like you don't have long to wait."

"I beg your pardon?"

"The bouquet."

"Oh, that. It's just an old wives tale." Both smiled.

"C'mon, let's go outside," Randall said, ushering her through the patio door.

On the patio, Lisa spun around, "I can't leave my aunt."

"Oh, yes, you can." Randall kissed her passionately. "I've missed you terribly."

Lisa's head was spinning and her pulse fluttered. The electrical sensations were overpowering. She was intoxicated with him. At last she managed, "Why haven't you called?'

"For the same reason as you. Stubborn. I have an immense ego," he joked. "I want you, Lisa."

"Here?"

"Be serious. Go with me to Galveston? I need to be alone with you." His voice was like a soft caress.

"Where's your car? I'll have to let my aunt know."

"I'll meet you outside in ten minutes."

Lisa was convinced she needed a cat scan, but continued, "Okay, ten minutes."

"Where are you are going?" Louise questioned over the noise of the party.

"To Galveston with Randall."

"You have my blessings." Louise embraced Lisa. "Go on and work it out with him. You've both been miserable."

"I will. Thanks, Louise. Where's Daniel?"

"Over there." Louise pointed.

Lisa moved in his direction. She pulled Daniel aside and whispered in his ear.

Daniel smiled. "Maybe you can straighten him out. He's been crankier than a porcupine without quills. Go on, gal. My son loves you, only he doesn't know it yet."

Lisa hugged the older man. "Congratulations," Lisa beamed. "You've got yourself a fine woman."

"I know. Now, go!"

Outside, Lisa climbed into Randall's car and pulled the door closed. Moments later, the Ferrari entered the Gulf Freeway.

"You won't be sorry." Smiling, Randall squeezed her hand.
The following hour was pensive on route to Galveston. Lisa was both anxious and exhilarated.

Presently his beach house came into view. Thank heaven!

Lisa stood in the doorway as Randall walked through the house flipping on lights as he went. Tugging at his tie, he threw it across a chair. Lisa noticed artwork had been added along with some area throw rugs, and figurines. The place reflected the owner. A house was not a home until it achieved a personality, she thought.

"At last! I thought we'd never arrive," Randall sighed. "Make yourself comfortable."

"I see you've added some touches," Lisa remarked appreciatively.

"I wanted it to have character."

Lisa wandered through the house, her eyes scanning the changes. Just as she turned, she almost collided with Randall. Silently, he appeared at her side.

Drawing her into his arms, he kissed her thoroughly. She looked as though, she needed to be kissed and often, he thought. Once more, the electrical sensations began. Randall knew he was in big trouble.

Lisa floated into the heavens. And he had only kissed her. You're in bad shape girl, she scolded. Who cares? Did she say that?

"We need to talk," Randall murmured.

"Now?"

"It can wait," he whispered.

His eyes locked with hers for an extended moment. Abruptly, he swept her into his arms. He climbed the stairs two at a time. He heaved a sigh as he gently laid her on the bed. Lisa allowed him to undress her. He fumbled with the zipper and the hooks of her brassiere.

"Touch me," he coaxed. He closed his eyes.

What's this around his middle? A cummerbund? It looked complicated to remove with all the tiny buttons. Men's clothing is as complicated as women's, she thought. Diligently, she worked at last, one, two, and three.

It was evident in his eyes, Randall missed her as much as she had him. Contacting flesh, Lisa moved her hands upward along his sides. Pausing briefly over his nipples, she traced each with a thumb until he moaned a throaty sound.

"Oh God, Lisa!" He threw his head back. "You don't know what you do to me." Withdrawing, he removed his pants.

"I think I have a good idea," she teased provocatively. "What do you want?"

"You," he responded, moving toward her.

"Take me, now."

Randall could wait no longer. He took her and the volcanic eruptions kissed the heavens, molten and consuming, rocketing forward, climbing, and swirling. Together, moving in unison, as one.

Lisa thought she had crossed the last hurdle, when they began again.

Much later, they slept intertwined.

When Lisa stirred, dragging an arm across the bed, she discovered it empty. She opened her eyes with a soft moan. Where was Randall? She raised on both elbows and looked around.

He stood on the veranda, clad only in faded jeans that caressed his body like a second skin. Thoughtfully, Randall's gaze swept Galveston Bay.

"Good morning," Lisa said stretching.

Randall turned and smiled. "Hello."

"Would you like breakfast?" she asked.

"No."

She swung her legs out of bed and made her way to the bathroom. "I'm going to bathe. See you in a few minutes," she said from the doorway.

He smiled. His gaze returned to the bay. Randall could hear the shower in the background. Should he tell her? He had been miserable this last week and restless. He knew he wanted to wake with her every day, but she had turned him down flat.

Each time they made love it was better, if possible than before. He was unaccustomed to being told no. He could never accept it. Randall discovered he could not live without Lisa. She brought sunshine and put the wind back in his sails. He admitted Lisa gave his life purpose. He admired her spirit and fortitude. He despised women with no life in them. Lisa brought a breath of fresh air into his life. Randall knew for the first time he loved her. He wanted to tell her, but he could not bring himself to mouth the words. He could hear her singing off-key in the shower, he smiled.

Minutes later, Lisa joined him on the veranda.

"If you keep whisking me off unexpectedly, I'll have to carry a change of clothes," she laughed. "This is all I could find to wear." She twirled.

"My shirt never looked better."

"I didn't bring any makeup," she pouted, mockingly.

"You look better without it or the shirt for that matter," he teased. Wrapping his arms around her waist, Randall's chest rested against her back.

"It's beautiful here," Lisa said wistfully.

"We could live here and commute to Houston." Randall kissed her neck.

She made a half turn and gazed up at him. His eyes met hers. He was teasing her, she thought -- testing. She shook her head.

"It's time we had that talk," he murmured.

"What's on your mind?" Lisa inquired as she settled into a chair in the living room. He looked as though he lost his favorite puppy, she considered.

"I want to explain some things to you. Perhaps it will help you to understand me," Randall began.

Lisa smiled.

"I grew up quite a rebel. I was headstrong, still am. I've had to depend on myself. My parents were rarely around. I must have attended every school in the U.S and a few in Europe. When I see something I want, I go after it. I'm unaccustomed to defeat. You know about my temper. I've known many women. Until now, I've held no interest in one woman. I don't believe in marriage," Randall finished. "I've seen too many end, bitterly."

"I'm the one that got away. I represent a challenge. Don't you understand that? I'm flattered and it would work for awhile."

"Like hell!" Randall glowered. "You don't understand." He rose from the sofa and walked toward the open sliding doors, his back to her.
"Explain it to me."

Randall's pulse pounded in his ears. Why couldn't she understand that he loved her? He wanted to protect her. His father once said, women wanted and needed to hear, syrupy declarations of affection. Randall could handle temporary relationships. This one scared the hell out of him.

He always considered women heartless. Lisa was a first, soft and vulnerable, yet strong-willed. She had shaken his concept of the opposite gender. In the past, he couldn't be sure if women were interested in him or his money.

"Randall?"

"Yes?" he replied, attempting to focus his attention.

"What about Clarissa?"

"Clarissa is a friend."

"She's in love with you."

"I haven't encouraged her," Randall began. "What was between us, was over long before we met. She refuses to face the truth."

"How long before you'll say the same about us?"

"You're not buying an appliance, Lisa. I offer no guarantees."

No way was she going to tell him how difficult this was for her. Lisa knew it would be too painful. "That's just it. I'm not buying any of this!" Lisa was on the verge of tears. His eyes softened. Was his expression bewilderment? She couldn't be sure.

"Are you in love with me?" Randall questioned.

"You're an incredible egomaniac!" Lisa accused, as she swiftly brought her palm to contact his face. "You have it all, don't you? But you're not happy!"

Randall was stunned. What did he expect? She had a right to be angry. He wanted a commitment from her, but offered none.

She stepped back.

"You're angry?" he said quietly.

"What do you want from me, Randall?" Lisa was emotionally spent.

"Everything." He kissed her like there was no tomorrow. Lisa was dizzy. Releasing her, he said, "I love you, Lisa."

"You what?" She was sure he had gone mad.

"I love you," Randall repeated with a broad smile, as if he'd climbed Mount Everest. "There I said it. It felt good."

Lisa was dumfounded.

"You never answered my question," he challenged.

"I always thought you knew."

"Tell me."

"I've loved you from the moment I saw you. I think I've been dazed ever since," Lisa admitted.

"What do you want to do about it?"

"Most people marry."

"I can't offer that option. Could you be happy living with me?"

"It looks as though we've reached an impasse," Lisa remarked.

"Were you intimate with Steven?"

"No," she said softly. "I couldn't because of you."

"Oh God, Lisa! If only I could be sure." He drew her to him.

"You're afraid! she exclaimed. "Why?"

"Sit down," Randall encouraged. "I've never told this to anyone. One of the few holidays I spent with my parents I remember hearing them argue. My father accused my mother of infidelity. She denied it. It seems she had a voracious appetite for men."

"How can you be sure?"

"Each time I returned home, the same old arguments cropped up," he confided. "I guess I hated the way she flaunted it at him. He was hen-pecked. He lived to please her."

Silence.

"Can you still love me?" Randall asked, reluctantly.

"None of this changes the way I feel about you," Lisa reassured. She drew him to her.

His bitterness and rebuke were understandable, she thought. Each had childhood scars that were slow to heal, she considered.

"Now do you understand?" Randall asked. "This is all I am capable of, right now. Trust me, my love?"

"Do you like children?" Lisa queried.

"Are you pregnant?" Randall muttered with a concerned expression.

"If I were?"

"I'd have to marry you."

"I don't think, I'd want you that way," Lisa stated.

"I would want to, if you are," Randall added.

"You have a real abhorrence to marriage," Lisa said, studying his expression.

"Fear," he supplied. "But I do love you. Do you plan to make us both miserable by refusing?"

"This is getting us nowhere," she muttered.

Randall swept Lisa into his arms and carried her to bed. He made slow, passionate love to her. Alas, they descended to earth once more. He was filled with a new purpose in life. He had to convince her he was no longer afraid.

"Lisa, I love you with all my heart and soul," Randall declared. "Will you marry me?"

"What about children?" Lisa asked softly.

"Are you sure that's what you want?"

"Oh, yes!" she cried as she clung to him. The words were

sweeter than any she had ever heard.

"Thank, heaven!" Randall sighed. "I couldn't bear to lose you."

Tears filled her eyes.

"Why are you crying?"

"I thought I would never hear those words!"
"I'll say them for the rest of our lives." Randall drew her into his arms. "Where were we?"

Lisa couldn't remember when she had been happier as they drove back to Houston. Randall just kept a silly smile on his face, she thought.

"It looks like there is something to those old wives tales," Lisa said playfully.

"What?"

"I caught the bridal bouquet, twice."

"Do you attend weddings in your spare time?" Randall teased.

"Louise is going to die when I tell her."

"My Dad will too," Randall admitted as he pulled into the Martin driveway. "Let's set a date?"

"October. A month's not forever," she reasoned. "After all, we have the rest of our lives."

"I would prefer Las Vegas. We could fly there, and get married. Then come back and tell everyone."

"Are you afraid you'll change your mind?" Lisa challenged.

"Never," Randall answered. "C'mon, let's go inside."
~****~

**Epilogue**

"I'll get it!" Randall shouted from the kitchen as the doorbell rang.

"Steven, it is good to see you," Randall said, smiling as he opened the door. "Who is the young lady?"

Once inside, Steven introduced, "Randall, this is Julie, my fiancée."

"Randall Barryman, pleased to meet you. My wife will be down in a few minutes. She's putting the baby to bed."

Steven and Julie were seated next to one another on the sofa and Randall took a chair across from them. "Well now tell me, how are things?" Randall offered. "Would you care for a drink?"

"Yes, that would be nice. Julie agreed to marry me last night," Steven said with enthusiasm.

"We'll toast the occasion when Lisa comes down," Randall suggested with a smile. "How are things at the advertising company?"

"Not bad, considering I have been in charge for a year now," Steven replied with a mischievous grin. "How is your father adjusting to being a grandfather?"

"He's never looked better. He and Louise are very happy. Both are doting grandparents," Randall commented.

"I thought I heard the door," Lisa said, descending the stairs. Kissing Steven's cheek, she asked with a puzzled expression, "What's going on here?" Lisa searched their faces to discover why everyone seemed to be smiling as if they shared a common secret.

"It seems Steven has decided to forfeit his bachelorhood in order to join the ranks. Julie, Mr. Ferguson's daughter has agreed to become Mrs. Steven Alexander," Randall supplied, lifting a glass to toast the happy couple.

"How wonderful, congratulations," Lisa responded by joining Randall's toast.

"Here's to Steven and Julie's happiness and forth coming marriage." Everyone lifted their glass.

"We're pleased you could join us for dinner," Randall said as Lisa nodded.

"Your home is lovely," Julie commented, glancing around the room. "I see you have a baby – a boy, I understand."

"Yes, he's eight months old. He gets cranky when its bedtime."

"Lisa, you look as though married life is agrees with you. You're putting on some weight," Steven said as he held Julie's hand, tightly. "Are you bored? I mean, since you gave up advertising for motherhood."

"Actually, I don't have much spare time with the baby and

house to take care of. I'm trying my hand at writing children's books."

"Shall we share our news, Lisa?" Randall asked teasingly. Everyone turned in a quandary toward Lisa.

"We found out today that we are going to have a second child." A flush appeared on Lisa's cheeks.

"Congratulations!" Steven said as he raised his glass indicating a second toast. "Here's to a healthy, happy baby girl this time!"

"May I see the baby?" Julie asked. "I just love babies."

Once the women returned from viewing the sleeping child, they joined the men downstairs.

"Your baby boy is sweet," Julie said, smiling.

"Yes. He looks just like his daddy," Randall boasted proudly.

"Men!" Lisa scolded mockingly.

"With the chestnut hair, I'm sure everyone must agree he favors his father," Julie said as Lisa filled their glasses.

"Yes, they do. He even has Randall's eyes," Lisa answered as she looked admiringly at her husband, standing beside her.

Squeezing her shoulder possessively, Randall kissed her neck. He turned his gaze to Steven and Julie as he said, "I hope you find as much happiness as we have. I've grown to love Lisa more each day."

~THE END~

ABOUT THE AUTHOR

Melisant Scott is an aficionada of the romance genre. She has enjoyed reading romance novels for several years, alas she decided to try her hand at writing. She hopes everyone enjoys reading, *Reluctant Heart*, a story about a love triangle. Everyone knows love triangles are always complicated -- somebody wins, and somebody loses. Melisant's hobbies include sailing, music, classic movies, her cats and her home is Texas.

To purchase other books by Melisant Scott on the internet visit: *Open Window Publications*. Most of her romance books are available in both paperback and digital (e-books) formats. Be sure to follow Melisant Scott on *Facebook* or *Twitter*. Watch for the release of her next book, *Forbidden Passion*.

Resources: facebook.com/scottmelisant ; twitter.com/melisantscott ; openwindowpublications.com ; melisantscott.org ; amazon.com/author/MelisantScott

www.ingramcontent.com/pod-product-compliance
Lightning Source LLC
Chambersburg PA
CBHW060422260626
47161CB00005B/1744